COLD

SUMMER

MY BROTHER'S KEEPER

A Novel by

Courtney B.

To submit a manuscript for our review,

email us at

submissions@majorkeypublishing.com

Chapter 1

August 4, 2016

It was a late summer night during a thunderstorm as I laid in my bed and stared out the window. My eyes were filled with tears and mind with terror as a bright lightning bolt flashed and struck a nearby tree, followed by the deep boom of thunder that rattled the glass in my windowpane. Although my heart raced by the combination of the two, it was the domestic dispute between my parents that took place in the very next room that frightened me the most.

"I hate you, Clarence! I'm sick of you always feeling like it's okay to do drugs and beat on me! I'm not having it anymore! Just get out! Get out of my fucking house!" my mom yelled as glass shattered against the wall.

"Shut the fuck up and tell me where you stashed the money! I don't give a fuck about none of that other shit you're talking about! I'll leave once you give me what I want!" my sorry excuse of a father answered as I could hear his large hand smack across my mom's face.

I helplessly laid flat on my back and averted my attention from the window to the ceiling. I clinched my fist as tight as I could and cried heavily. I tried to pray, but it still didn't drown out the argument or the thump of my mother's petite body as it got slammed aggressively against the wall.

"Chance, it's okay, Pops on that needle again, that's all," my twin brother, Choyce, said as he looked over from his bed that was right across from mine. Our dad had relapsed back into his heroin addiction.

Although he would quit from time to time, his abusive behavior worsened whenever he decided to stop or just started back. It seemed like the only time our family could deal with him was when he was completely on the drugs, therefore, I wished he never stopped.

"Just get some rest, lil' bruh, it will all be over soon. Plus, your first day of high school is tomorrow," he continued as he handed me my pillow that fell on the floor.

"Man! I hate him, bro! I wish he would just do so much of that shit that he'd overdose and die!" I yelled out of frustration caught up in my emotions.

"I know, Chance. Trust me, I feel the same way, just chill though, get some rest. We need for you to be as focused as you can. After all, you're going to be the bread winner of the family one day, Mr. Future NFL hall-of=famer. Think fast!" he said then tossed a football my way in the pitch dark.

"Aww, shit! Damn bro, you hit me in my eye. Why'd you just throw it, knowing I couldn't see?" I questioned and covered my face with both hands, only to hear our bedroom door kicked open. As the door banged against the wall, I could see my dad cut the light on through the cracks of my fingers.

"The fuck is you two still up for? You'd better close them mothafuckin eyes and get rest! Y'all got school in the morning!" my dad demanded as he stood at the threshold of the door in nothing but his boxers and wife beater.

"You mean, close our eyes like you just closed mom's?" Choyce questioned as he covered his face with his blanket, only to get drug from out the bed by his ankles.

"The fuck you just say to me! You want some too?" Dad said as picked Choyce up by his neck and slammed him against the wall.

"Get off my brother!" I yelled as I jumped to my feet and threw my football at the back of my dad's head. It just bounced off, and he turned towards me with what looked like fire in his eyes.

"Sit yo ass down, lil' nigga!" was all heard before, I received a back hand that knocked my lights out.

I was dazed as I stood to my feet, I had a knife hide under my mattress. I pretended as if I held my face as I reached for it. My dad continued to beat on my brother as I secured it in my hand. Then, while his back was still towards me, I rushed my dad.

"I fucking hate you!" I screamed out as I stabbed him in the back.

"Chance! What are you doing?" he questioned as

9

I continued to stab him repeatedly.

"Die! Die! Why don't you just die?" I said as his blood splattered and tears filled my eyes, I used all my strength to stab him until he fell to the ground.

"Chance, stop don't do me like this! Please! Stop! Chance, Chance, Chance!" I heard my father yell, followed by a smack to the face as I regained consciousness.

"Where am I?" I questioned as I looked around only to find out, I had been knocked out cold from my dad's rough, oversized hand and had been laid out on my bedroom floor all night. Once focused, I realized that I had dreamed the murder of my father. Although, I was relived, it was still bittersweet.

*****

As Choyce and I sat at the breakfast table, the smell bacon and eggs filled the room. I closed my eyes and deeply inhaled the aroma. I heard my mom place our plates on the table. I opened them to thank her and say grace, but the instant I saw her badly beaten face, I was at a loss of appetite.

"You two hurry up and eat, I'ma drop you off before I head to work," said my dad as he gave Choyce and I a demanding stare.

"I'm not hungry." I murmured, pushing the plate forward and turning my head, disgusted at the sight of that man.

"Chance, eat up, baby. You too, Choyce, I can't have you two going to school on empty stomachs," I heard my mom say in a sweet tone.

I always admired her strength, no matter what she went through. She held her head high and carried herself like a queen. She would say from time to time to Choyce and me,

"Boys, if you ever find yourselves in love, make sure you know that woman's worth. Treat her right, support her dreams, and tend to her every need. And she'll give you the world in the palm of your hands." Even though she was treated like she was worthless by my piece of shit father.

"What? You aren't hungry! Ain't this ah bitch? I bet, I won't provide another meal for you ungrateful sons

11

of bitches!" Dad yelled as he took our plates and slammed them into the wall.

"Now, get y'all shit and let's go!" he demanded with anger as he grabbed his work coat off his chair and proceeded towards the living room, only to get stopped in his tracks by a phone call. He pulled his phone out of his pocket then answered in a frustrated tone.

"Hello!" Choyce and I stood in silence as we witnessed how our father's facial expression frown up even more.

"I'm under an investigation for what!" he yelled as he clinched the cellphone tighter in his hand, then walked completely into the living room for more privacy.

"You two just have a seat, I'll take you to school once I get ready for work," my mother said as she just wiped the mess off the kitchen counter, stove, and sink dad had made. She then pushed her and my dad's chair under the table and walked towards the living room.

Choyce and I just sat quietly as our father yelled to the top of his lungs, at whoever he was on the phone with.

"What? Job abandonment! Since when have I ever left without letting my punk ass supervisor know? Huh! I can't believe you dirty mothafuckahs are just going to lie on and fire me like this. I have a wife and two fucking kids! How in the fuck are we supposed to make it out here?" Dad questioned in a raged outburst.

"Now don't act surprised, when I come up there to pick up my last check and shoot the entire place up! Because you all chose to play with my livelihood!" he threatened as my mom snatched the phone out of his hand and quickly hung up.

"It's okay, baby. You don't have to go there with them! I still have my job and just got a three dollar raise, so everything will work out. You'll find another job just don't lose hope because it's not the end of the world. A violent reaction like this is only making matters worse. I'm telling you; everything will be okay—" Mom pleaded but got silenced mid-sentence due to a back hand across her face.

"Bitch! Shut the fuck up, how in the fuck do you know it's going to be okay? I don't have a fucking job!

I'm the breadwinner of this household, I don't give a fuck about your funky ass three dollar raise!" he yelled as he looked down on my mom then over at us.

I was enraged by the way he kept disrespecting my mom in front of me. I looked over and saw a knife on the kitchen counter. My dream that I stabbed him to death came back to me, it was a now or never moment for me. My adrenalin rushed my body, but when I got up to walk towards it, my legs wobbled. I was too nerves to act on my instincts. Choyce looked over at me, he then saw what I was headed for and grabbed my wrist.

"Just chill out, bro, he'll get what's coming to him one day," he whispered as I sat back down. By then, my mom had begun to scream out at my dad.

"You're right, Clarence! You shouldn't give a fuck about my accomplishment as a black woman, that's making her dream come true. The fact that I worked hard, to get to where I am while dealing with your bullshit for all these years, hoping one day you'd change. But all you've done is made matters worse and developed a drinking and drug problem." She'd reached her breaking point. Choyce and I looked at each other with our mouths wide open. We'd never heard our mom stand on dad the way she did, but it made us proud of her.

"You're sick, Clarence! You need help, you can take your stupid ass up to that place and act a fool if you want to. But watch how quick you'll see, they'll have a special place in the county jail, for ignorant people such as yourself," Mom said as she walked over to the kitchen counter then turned back towards him.

"Bitch! Say another mothafuckin word, and I'll knock your teeth clean out your mouth!" my dad said aggressively. He walked over to her and reached to grab Mom by the collar of her shirt with both hands.

"You'd better learn how to stay in a woman's place." As he grabbed hold of her shirt, he quickly let go and took a step back. My mom had the knife I was about to get, pointed right at his stomach.

"I've had enough of your womanizing, abusive, chauvinistic ways. I'm sick of it! And before I allow you to put your hands on me again, in front of my kids, I'd rather gut you to death and watch you bleed out by my feet. Now, get out of my house, you damn, fool!" Mom demanded, and Dad continued to walk backwards with his hands in the air.

"Okay, I'm gone, but you'll regret that you ever pulled a weapon out on me. Just wait and see." Dad made his threat, grabbed his coat, and stormed out of the house as he slammed the door behind himself. Mom instantly drooped to her knees and cried aloud.

"I'm so sorry you two have to go through this," she sobbed and laid the knife down on the kitchen floor. We quickly rushed over and wrapped our arms around her as we attempted to comfort her.

"It's okay, Mom, don't cry," I whispered in her ear, then kissed her forehead.

"Yeah, Mom, you're going to be straight. We got this, just the three of us," Choyce assured as he used his shirt to wipe the tears from her cheeks.

My dad made good on his promise, by going up to his job and acting a fool. They locked him right up just as my mom warned. He only did twenty-four hours, but when he got home, he started hanging at gambling shacks

16

and ticket houses. He ran into a few of his old friends and continued to use heavy drugs.

He eventually got himself locked back up, but that time, the courts gave him two years in prison.

Mom went back to school and picked up where she'd left off. Just a year later, she finished and received her M.D. She became a Doctor of Medicine for Eli Lilly's and made good money.

She purchased our first home in her old neighborhood, and it was right around the corner from our school. Choyce and I decided to walk to and from there, being that mom's new work schedule conflicted with our school hours.

Chapter 2

One year later

It was my sophomore year, and I had already made a name for myself playing football. I was the varsity starting runback and starting linebacker. I stood out to my peers because of my choice to be different. Everyone around me seemed to be into the street life. Therefore, they came to school and looked as if it were a fashion show.

Not me though, I took school seriously. Mom always questioned as to why I chose to wear the same clothes and offered to take me shopping plenty of times. But each time, I told her no and to save her money for my college tuition.

"Hey, Chance!" Channy yelled out as I walked past her locker.

We'd met each other in middle school, and we clicked from day one. Over the years, we talked about everything. She shared stories with me, about her upbringing that she never shared with anyone else, and I the same. So, I must admit, my feelings were a little crushed when I found out she had gotten into a relationship.

"What's good, shorty?" I questioned back with a shy grin and stopped to spark a conversation.

Ever since middle school, out of all the girls, I'd always liked her the most. She was different and was inspired to be a fashion designer one day, but she wasn't into flashy clothes or hanging in large groups just to get attention like all the others. She was still popular in her own way, and that's what attracted me to her the most. I looked at her like the female version of me because all our similarities.

"Oh, nothing, I just wanted to tell you, that was a good game you had on Friday. I meant to tell you, Saturday, but I don't have your new number. Soo, what's up with that, bruh?" she questioned with a bashful smile as she playful nudged my shoulder with her fist, then cuffed her books close to her chest with both arms.

"Well, I didn't think you wanted it, considering you were dating the homie and all," I replied as I shrugged my shoulders in a nonchalant manner.

"Boy, stop it, you know these niggas ain't shit. So, enough with the jokes," she stated without cracking a grin.

"Oh, my bad but if you really want my number, I'll text it to you right now," I replied in relief.

That was another thing I loved about Channy, even though she was smart, she had the mentality of a savage. After all she told me she'd been through, I couldn't blame her. Right when I got my cell out my pocket, I had gotten rudely interrupted.

"Here this niggah is right here!" my guy, Sam, yelled out from down the hallway as he and a few other players from my team came rushing towards me. Sam was the loudmouth type, but he was heart of our team. He was something like Ray Lewis the way, he hyped us up in the locker room before each game. We would get so geeked up, we'd go out and crash the opposing team.

"So, how does it feel, my nigga?" he questioned and held up the sports section of the newspaper. I read the headline and it was all about me, having 1500 yards rushing by my ninth game. It also had my defensive stats, but I was so amazed by my rushing yardage, I couldn't pay attention.

"Yo! Is this shit real?" I reacted with excitement.

"Nigga, this shit is as real as it gets. You the one. bro! And we're now number one in our division!" JT, one of my other teammates, intervened in a hype manner, which added to the moment.

"Oh, shit! I gotta go show my bro!" I mentioned as I hurried to walk away. I was so caught up in reading the article, I walked right past Channy by mistake. When I got to Choyce's locker, he had about seven people gathered around him.

"Aye, lil' bruh, come here right quick!" he yelled and gestured the hand motion.

Ever since we'd moved into our new house, Choyce had been hanging with our next door neighbor, Justin, a lot. They'd been best friends since grade school, so they were close like brothers. Early last year, Choyce started buying a lot of new clothes and counted out large amounts of money all the time. When I questioned him, why he hid his money or kept all his new clothes over Justin's house, he'd say just focus on my schoolwork and football, he knew what he was doing. So, I left it alone.

"What's up, Chance? Let me see your backpack right quick," he asked as I stepped through the crowd, dropped it from my shoulder, and handed it to him. He hurried to stuff some money in it, zipped it up, and handed it back to me.

"Link wit me at your locker after school. I want you to walk with me and Justin on our way home. I got something that I gotta talk to you about," Choyce whispered as he shut his locker and put his arm around my shoulder.

"No problem, bro, but check this out," I said and handed him the sports section. The smile that came across his face was the one of a proud father. He stopped walking, so he could read it, and that was the best feeling in the world to me.

"No shit! Congratulations! Yo! I'm hanging this on my wall as soon as we get home!" he said with excitement. We shook up then went to our classes.

*****

After school was over, I linked up with Choyce at my locker like he'd asked. He'd always been twenty steps ahead of life, and for every level of knowledge he obtained, he made sure I was up on game with him.

"Bro, I'm telling you, we're going to be up on ah hundred bands in no time fucking with this shit," Justin said as I walked up on them in mid conversation.

"Off top, my nigga, real shit, but we gotta move smooth around this bitch. We got too many niggas watching and plotting. I heard one of them opp ass niggas we got into it with last week was talking about robbing us and shit. They just don't know, we bout whatever they bout. Dumb shit, we got that for'em, real talk," Choyce addressed in a stern manner.

"Nah, for real," Justin replied. Justin was just a cool cat; he had all the ladies, always dressed fresh than a bitch, and kept money in his pocket. He started teaching Choyce some things and people had begun to hate on them. I loved it though and was confused as to why others didn't.

"What good, fellas?" I questioned as I tried not to show any signs worry.

"Not shit, lil' bruh. We're on our way home, but I gotta show you a different route. We got some opps on some bullshit with me and Justin. But I didn't want them to get us mistaken because this has nothing to do with you," Choyce answered as he looked me in the eyes with concern.

"Come on, Choyce, lets go. We gotta make a move before it's too late," Justin said and led the way.

I swear as we walked through the hallways, it was like I was walking with two celebrities. All the girls called out to Justin and Choyce; all the guys showed them love. I considered it an honor as they were greeted all the way, until we made it to the side doors of the school.

When we walked out, the sun shined bright. I looked up and white clouds filled the sky. It was a beautiful day, the leaves on the trees were tuning orange, telling me fall was on its way. It was a little breezy, so I decided to put my hood on. No sooner than I did about five car loads of people pulled up from out of nowhere.

"Stand behind us, Chance," Justin demanded as he and Choyce stood in front of me.

"The fucks up now!" I heard someone yell from the first car. As all the doors opened, and a total of fourteen dudes got out their cars.

"Aye, these them bum ass niggas, who swear they doing the most and making money in our hood!" someone yelled from the driver's side of their car.

"Bums? Nigga, we the hottest in the city, that's why all y'all bitches love us, fuck niggah!" Choyce said as he threw his arms up, in a what's up motion.

"You scary as niggahs act like, y'all don't know how to make no money! So, we just took over to show you how it's done. Really, y'all should be thankful!" he continued.

"Thankful? Nigga! Do you know who the fuck I am? Check this shit out though, if I catch you two trying to sell in the hood again! On God! I'm ah blast both you bitches straight up," the driver of the first car said as he pulled a handgun from under his hoodie.

"Man, fuck that shit! All you niggas got all them guns, talking the most shit, but I bet y'all won't kill nothing. Y'all act like y'all ready to shoot, but if one of us falls today, are any of you bitches ready for our retaliation that's going down tonight!" Justin yelled as he postured up in a brave manner, but all he did was provoke the situation as three more people pulled out their guns and cocked them back.

"The fuck you just say, Lil nigga!" some older guy, who looked to be at least twenty-five, said as he took a few steps closer then pointed his weapon at us.

I was nervous, it was the first time I had ever had a gun pulled out on me, yet alone four of them. All I could do was keep my eyes on Choyce and Justin. I just wished they'd leave us alone, so we could go home, but that didn't seem like it was going to happen.

"I'm just saying, all you niggas out here, but it's just the three of us. And ain't none of y'all got the balls to go hands up?" Choyce questioned out of confusion as he looked at everyone that surrounded us from our left to our right.

"Fuck them, let's get this shit over wit and ride out. Before someone calls the law, you got warrants, O.G.," one of them suggested to the older guy with his gun pointed on us, once he noticed bus loads full of students and teachers on looking.

"Nah, put the guns away. This lil nigga got a point, aye, Noah! Come bump with this bitch ass nigga right quick. We'll handle the gunplay later," the O.G. ordered as Choyce and Noah squared up to fight one on one.

"Yeah, fuck nigga, you got what you asked for. Now what—" Noah blurted out but was cut short from his conversation because Choyce hit him so hard, it echoed throughout the bus parking lot. All the rest of the kids on the buses yelled out, "Damn!"

Choyce kept getting his punches off, and it made all the other guys that pulled up so deep, look bad. That's when someone fired a gun shot in the air.

"Choyce! Let's go!" Justin yelled out as we all three took off running. As we did, a few more shots rang out. We ran so fast, that we made it a couple blocks away in what seemed like a matter of seconds. We ended up cutting-through the mini junkyard, behind a car garage at the end of the ally not too far from our house.

"Damn, lil' bruh, you okay?" Choyce questioned. He was bent down and held his knees as he tried to catch his breath.

"Yeah bro, but what was that about?" I answered then questioned back. I was in fear for my life and confused as to what had just happened.

"Nothing, bro. I just whooped that weak ass nigga, for all that shit he was talking!" Choyce explained.

"Trust me, Chance, it's not your fault, I'll explain later. It's just niggas don't know how to mind their own fucking business! Hopefully, this shit over with!" he continued.

"What you do you mean, what's over?" I questioned more. My heart pounded heavily, and what Choyce had said, didn't make any since to me.

"Listen, lil' bruh! I said, I'll explain later. Justin, you good, bro? Choyce questioned as we both looked around but didn't see him.

"Justin!" Choyce yelled out, but he was still nowhere in sight.

"Yo! Justin!" Choyce yelled again, and there was still no reply. Right then, I felt my heart drop. It was an unusual breeze that came from out of nowhere. It led back towards the direction that we had just ran from.

"Aye, Justin!" Choyce called out in a humbler tone. By that time, tears had filled his eyes as we started to back track.

Choyce had begun to let his tears flow, and I braced myself. Because I knew I wasn't ready for the sight I was about to see.

"Man, no. No! No! No! Please not yet, this shit ain't real!" Choyce pled. As we walked closer, to the school I knew something wasn't right. As the police had already arrived and just begun to put the yellow tape up.

I stopped in my tracks because I'd never seen a dead body before. Justin was laid on his stomach, with his arm forward as if he'd tried to reach for us.

"Justin! Bro!" Choyce yelled. He tried to run and pick him up but was tackled by a nearby police officer.

"This is a crime scene! What are you doing?" the officer yelled in explanation. Choyce put up so much of a fight, that he had to get restrained. I couldn't move, I didn't know if I should cry or help my brother.

"Justin! Justin!" Choyce yelled repeatedly. He spazzed so hard, the police had to pick him up and place in the back of a police car. By then, I'd dropped to my knees. I looked up towards the sky, and for the first time, I cried out.

"God, what's going on!" It was sad, I'd never in a million years, would've thought I would witness, something as tragic as that was. Not too long after, a police officer came over and helped me up, then escorted me to his vehicle."

"What's your name, kid?" he questioned as we walked me over to his car door.

"I'm Chance Coleman," I answered and sobbed. I just couldn't figure out what Choyce and Justin making money, had to do with anything. I didn't understand at all, I mean, they made money and dressed fresh all the time. What was so wrong that that? What made people hate them so much, that someone had to die for it?

"Don't worry, Chance, you're not under arrest. We just heard that you and your brother, witnessed this shooting, and I must take you in for questioning. Once we get your statement and call your parents, you'd be free to go," he assured as I got in the car.

*****

Choyce and I were taken to the juvenile detention center and placed in two different rooms. There, we were questioned by detectives.

"Chance Coleman, how's it going?" one of the detectives questioned. He entered the room with my backpack in his hand, he then sat it down by his foot. He pulled the chair out from the table and sat directly across from me. The entire time, I had my hands palms flat on the table. It felt as if they had the heat on, how I sweated profusely.

The detective just stared at me for a few minutes. I couldn't keep eye contact with him because of the awkward silence. When he noticed I was scared, he

31

then started his investigation. I had begun to shake a little. It was from the fact that I was in an investigation room alone, with a grown white man, I didn't even know from Adam.

"What' wrong, Chance? You seem a little uneased right now?" he questioned. He tossed a notebook on the table and placed his pen on top of it. He sat back in his chair, loosened up his tie, then crossed his leg.

"Nuh—nothing," I stuttered. I was lost, I couldn't understand, why things turned out the way they did that day. First, we were surrounded by a large group of people, with their guns drawn out on us. Then, once we defended ourselves, we got chased and shot at? I was even more lost, when I saw someone that I knew, laid out dead as the fatal ending.

"Well, let's just start from the beginning. From what I was told, you and your brother, and friend were starting trouble with a group of guys that didn't even belong to your school. Am I correct?" he questioned. He uncrossed his leg, sat up straight in his chair, picked up his pen and clicked it.

"No, sir, you're not correct. Those guy's started problems with us. We were minding our own business on our way home when they pulled up on us. They got out their cars, talking about things we had no idea about. They pulled out their guns once we defended ourselves, that's when we ran, and they started shooting," I explained as I began to cry. I was frightened by the flash backs, yet saddened by the death of Justin, and I just wanted to go home.

"Chance, listen to me. I am your only hope, if you ever want to see the day light again. You should tell me the truth right now. Because I have witnesses that say different. So, I'm going to give you one last chance. What was this about?" The detective had me at a loss for words. I just sat there with my mouth wide open as my entire life flashed before my eyes.

"Why aren't I ever going to see the day light again?" I questioned. That's when the detective stood to his feet, picked up my backpack unzipped and dumped it out on the table. I had forgotten all about the money, Choyce had put in there earlier that day. I didn't even know how to explain.

"Tell me, the truth, Chance! I believe you stole this money from one of those guys. and they found out who you were and what school you went to!" he yelled. He then walked over and stood beside me. I was still looking forward scared and confused. "Was I responsible for this?" I had begun to question myself as he continued to rant.

"In return, they drove up to your school, looking for retaliation! They caught you trying to sneak out the side entrance! Once confronted, you lied and not only put your life in danger but every other student in that school!" The more the detective had gotten infuriated, the more I saw Justin on the ground as he reached for help. That's when reality hit me. Justin was dead. I had a nervous breakdown.

I cried uncontrollably, and when I closed my eyes, it was like I could see him. So, I then tried to extend my hand.

"Justin, take my hand! Follow me!" I screamed out and started to reach back. I couldn't feel his hand, so I tried again.

"Take my hand and stand up, Justin!" It didn't work, and at that point, I lost all control of my emotions. I couldn't believe, I was the reason behind Justin's death, and I needed for him to forgive me.

"I'm sorry, I didn't mean to get you killed! Please, forgive me!" I fell out my chair on to the floor and balled up. I started rocking and crying harder.

"Chance, I'm sorry, I believe you. Come on, get up," the detective said as he reached down and put his hand on my shoulder. I'd never seen a dead body before, but to hear it was all my fault, broke me spiritually.

"What's going on in here!" my mom screamed as she busted into the room and saw the detective stood over me while I was on the floor, balled up crying.

"Ma'am, I can explain, I just wanted to know why--" he attempted to explain but was cut short by some older black man that entered the room with my mom.

"Detective, I'm sure you're aware that questioning a minor without their parents' consent is prohibited by law in the state of Indiana, don't you?" the man questioned as he sat a briefcase on the table.

"Chance, come here, baby, Get up," Mom said as she kneeled to help me up.

"Mom, I'm sorry. I didn't mean to get anyone killed. I just don't know, what I did," I pled out of confusion. As I opened my eyes, I saw Choyce, my mom, and the older guy that questioned the detective. He had a bald head and wore a nice three-piece suit.

"Shh, it's okay, baby. What did you do to him?" my mom yelled to the detective as she held my head on her chest and covered my ear with both hands.

"Ma'am, once again, I'm truly sorry. I just noticed he had a large amount of cash in his backpack. I was just trying to make sure that wasn't the motive behind those cold-hearted thugs' acts of violence," the detective explained as he raised his hands like he was under arrest.

"Well, I'm Mr. McFarland, and I'm acting as Mrs. Coleman's family attorney. From now on if you have any further questions, you will first speak to me," the man addressed in a professional manner as he opened his briefcase, took out a business card, and gave it to the detective.

"Are we free to go?" my mom's friend questioned.

"Yes, I have no further questions. You are free to go." Mr. McFarland walked over to my backpack, placed everything back in it, then handed it to my mom. He then closed his briefcase.

"I'm sorry, kid," the detective apologized once again and extended his hand. My mom wrapped her arm around my shoulder and gave him a cold stair as we walked out the room.

On our way out the detention center, Mr. McFarland led us towards his SUV it was an all-black 2018 Suburban Denali with dark tints all the way around.

"Are you two, okay?" Mr. McFarland asked as he stood by the passenger side, then used his remote key to start it and unlock the doors.

"Yeah, we're good," Choyce said as he opened the back door, jumped in, and climbed over so I could get in too. I noticed how when mom reached for her door,

McFarland hurried to open it for her.

"Make sure you pull your coat all the way in," he suggested then shut her door. I watched him as he walked around to the back of his SUV. He opened the rear door, placed his briefcase in the back, then took off his coat, and hung it on a hanger.

He was different from my dad; I noticed that he treated my mom with respect. I looked in the front seat, and mom smiled from ear to ear. I never saw her smile like that before. Right then, the driver side door opened, and he got in.

"Are you hungry?" he looked over and questioned mom. She shook her head no.

"What about you two, are you hungry?" he asked as he adjusted his rearview.

"I couldn't eat right now if I wanted to, but thanks for asking," I answered, then looked over at Choyce as he laid his seat back and put his arm on the rest, then hand on his chin.

Choyce had hawk eye's on Mr. McFarland, and I understood why. My dad did mom wrong in front of us for so many years. He just felt like he had to protect her. I picked up a different vibe from him though, and I knew he was the one my mom should be around.

On our way home, mom seemed to be okay. But as soon as we made it a few blocks up from the house, she busted into tears.

"Tell me the truth okay? I only want the truth. Choyce, you have jewelry and clothes that I have no idea where it came from. Chance, you're walking around with over two thousand dollars in your backpack," she questioned as she wiped tears from her eyes.

"I just picked you two up from juvenile, after you witnessed your best friend's murder. You just don't know how worried I was, when I received that phone call. I thought they were going to tell me one of you had gotten killed," she explained and broke down some more. Mr. McFarland pulled over and parked, then put his hand on mom's shoulder.

"It's going to be okay, just relax," he suggested, but mom wasn't going for it.

"No, it's not going to be okay! I need some

answers, and I need them now!" Mom cried so hard, she could hardly talk.

"Listen, fellas, I know it's kinda hard to talk in front of me. But I'm your mom's friend and I have her back. Being that you two are her sons, I have your backs too. I know, I was introduced as Mr. McFarland, but you can call me Troy. I'm from this same neighborhood and I grew up in the gang life. I had strips out here, but I turned them in for this tie that I have on. After I witnessed my own brother wrongfully convicted, for a crime he didn't commit," Mr. McFarland intervened.

I was about to speak but, as soon I leaned forward, Choyce spoke up for us.

"Mom, it's okay, the guys that pulled up on us, had us mixed up, we didn't do anything wrong. Kids our age are acting worse than grown men. So, there's going to be a lot of things that just happen," Choyce explained. He then put his hands on his head out of frustration, closed his eyes tight, and leaned back. I could tell Justin's face flashed in his mind, but he kept his cool.

"Mom, I promise you that Chance and I, go to

school every day. And you have my word that we're going to graduate. I promise, so don't cry," Choyce regained his focus and finished. We reached over each side of her seat and placed our hands on her shoulder. She then put hers on top of ours.

"I know you two are, I believe you're going to be just fine. And I'm glad to see that you're being, responsible, young, well-dressed men. If you are doing anything that you shouldn't be, then please, just stop doing it for me today, okay?" she requested. She then let go of our hands and wiped the tears from her face. Mr. McFarland put the car back in drive then pulled off.

We were a few houses down from our house, I saw someone on our front porch. When we pulled up into the driveway, it was my dad. He managed to get out a year early due to good behavior, but the sight of him had my heart filled with fear.

"Is that him?" Mr. McFarland questioned as he as he parked in the driveway.

"Yes, it is," mom answered. Then buried her head to her hand and tried to shake it off as if it were all a dream.

"It's ok, I'll call and check on you later. I got a lot of work to do anyway," he said as he looked over at mom then back towards us.

"It was nice to finally meet you two. Although, I didn't expect it to be on these terms. At least you now know who I am, and what it is I do for a living," he addressed then turned back to my mom. Her smile came right back, and I felt relieved. She was around someone who truly cared for her.

"Thank you, Tory, and I will talk to you shortly," mom replied. Mr. McFarland opened his door, got out, and walked around to my mom's door. I looked up to see my dad's reaction, and he was just as stunned, once he opened it for her

"Boys!" mom called as she got out.

"Thank you, Mr. McFarland." I said, then got out and stood next to mom.

"Yeah, right on, good looking out," Choyce also commented. He got out and walked around the car, then stood in front of me and mom. I was surprised to see him extend his hand.

"Anytime, you two, and don't forget. I come from this place too, so no matter what it is you find yourselves into, I could probably relate. Don't be afraid to reach out."

"Who is this nigga!" my dad yelled from the porch. Mr. McFarland just stood in front of his SUV, with his hand over his fist. He had a smile on his face as we walked up towards the house.

"Who is that?" he questioned, in a calmer tone once my mom walked past him to unlock the door.

"Ask him, he's right there," she answered. She looked back then smiled as she got her keys out her purse.

Mr. McFarland got in his SUV then pulled off. Dad continued to question mom as they walked in the house. Choyce stopped and looked over at Justin's house. He was in a blank stare; I'd never seen him so thrown off before. But it was due to pain. I was saddened myself, so I stayed out there with him.

"Are you okay, bro?" I questioned. I walked over and stood right next to him.

"Yeah, I'm straight, lil' bruh, but my life is about to get real serious, and I need you to have my back." After he answered, he turned to look me in the eyes. He extended his hand to do our handshake, but the expression on his face was as if he'd become heartless. I didn't know what he meant, I just shook my head yes, and we walked into the house.

Chapter 3

Senior Year

It was going on three years since Justin had passed, and Choyce's life had taken a turn for the worst. Nobody could talk to him; he just came and went as he pleased. He didn't respect for anyone or anything. He told me to have his back, but I didn't know where to start. He had missed so much school his junior year, that even he couldn't believe we still ended up seniors together. I was worried and prayed nothing bad happened to him, but I had to focus on my own dreams.

I had almost every D-1 college in the United States, scouting to recruit me. My mom had already returned seven letters to major universities, and they all offered me full-ride scholarships.

It was the beginning of fall, and I noticed it was cold enough to see my breath as left the school building. I zipped up my North Face jacket and pulled my hood over my head. Water puddles and fallen leaves were everywhere. I had on my dark brown suede Timberlands, and I didn't want to ruin them, so I decided to take a shortcut.

I made it few blocks before I turned into the ally close to my house. The city had just repaved it, so I took that way. A way down, I saw Choyce cut though a yard, so I yelled his name. He couldn't hear me, so I sped up my walk. When I finally caught up to him, I noticed that he'd stopped between some houses.

He was in the middle of a conversation with Justin's uncle, who was dope fiend. I was going to announce my presence, but what I overheard made me stop in my tracks. So, I stood at the edge of the garage.

"Man, fuck all that! I'm not trying to hear, none of that shit! This nigga killed my nephew! Your brother! I now know for a fact it was him, and he has to die tonight!" the uncle yelled in an outrage.

"Fuck it, then, Unk, if you know it's him for sure. Then he must die tonight like you said. But what's up with the money part again?" Choyce answered, which made my heart drop. I'd just heard him say, he was about to help commit a murder robbery.

"Listen, nephew, every time I leave out the front door, that safe is always cracked. The nigga has at least fifty grand in it. Like I told you, I'll take care of the hard part, all you have to do is get the money," Justin's uncle explained, with the use of aggressive hand gestures.

"Are you sure it's fifty bands in there, Unk?" Choyce questioned as he rubbed his hands together.

"Honestly, I don't know, nephew. But what I do know is my SSI checks dropped to only $450 a month. Because of that, I'm barely making it out here," Justin's uncle explained.

"Don't get me wrong! That fuck nigga's money won't ever replace Justin's life, but it's been two and a half, going on three years, since he's been gone. And I'll be damned if he thinks, he's going to enjoy life for another day! While my nephew is laid six-feet beneath the ground!" Justin's uncle shouted then looked down at the leaves by his feet and kicked some to the side. Choyce just nodded his head in agreeance.

"I feel you, Unk, so what's the play?" Choyce continued to question. I could see his face clear and could tell he had a tinge of concern.

"Listen, the safe is in the first room by the front door, right underneath a window. The window is big enough for you and your brother to climb in with the two duffle bags, you said you had. You two should be able to fill both the bags up with whatever amount is in it. Once I feel you two had enough time to finish, I'll do my part, and we can get the fuck on," Justin's uncle further explained.

I instantly had gotten cold feet; I couldn't believe Choyce involved me in what he had going on. My entire future was on the line. I had a lot to lose if something went wrong. I found myself at a catch twenty-two. But although I was nervous, I made my brother a promise that I was going to have his back. So, I had to quickly get over my fears before nightfall.

"I'm going to be in the back room. He usually let's me buy and use my drugs there, but not tonight. I'll create a diversion by talking loudly and cracking jokes like I do. I'll keep my act going long enough, to block out any extra bumping around that y'all might do," he continued as he cracked open a beer then lit a cigarette.

"Say less, Unk, it's ah play then. But man, check this shit out. I'm going to bring my lil' bro in for this, one time. This isn't his life, and I don't want this for him. After this, if you see him on the streets, don't even look his way. I don't give a fuck if I'm around or not. Don't try me, if you know what's good for you," Choyce cautioned as he stared Justin's uncle eye to eye, with his fist balled up.

No matter where Choyce's life was headed, I knew he loved me and would do whatever to protect me. That's why I was so confused, when he included in something so dangerous.

"Calm down, nephew. I get it," he answered, with his head cocked to the side, one eye squelched, and his lit cigarette cliched between his lips.

"But on a lighter note, how's your dad doing? I heard he got out a couple years ago, and I ain't seen that nigga yet," Justin's uncle inquired to change the subject.

"Man! Fuck that nigga! He thinks, I'm going for all that, *prison made me change my life* bullshit. But after that niggah kept putting his hands on my mom for all them years, I don' trust him around her or us! And really, all this extra talking is irrelevant, let's get back to the money," Choyce responded in anger.

"Say less, nephew," Justin's uncle replied. He then picked up his four pack of Colt 45 from off the ground, cuffed it under his arm, then walked in my direction.

I didn't want them to think I was eavesdropping, so I quickly made my presence known.

"What's good, bro, Unk?" I questioned. As I reached my hand out, so Choyce and I could do our handshake, but I shook uncontrollably.

"What's good, youngster?" Justin's uncle said. He then lifted his head to the sky and walked right past me. He probably felt how hard Choyce looked upside his head.

"What's good, lil' bruh? Are you okay? Why are you shaking, did somebody fuck with you on the way home?" he questioned as he looked over my shoulder.

"Nah, it's just cold as fuck out here," I

answered. I had a bad feeling about what I overheard, so I decided to try and talk him out of it.

"Bro, I got this new playbook. It's for our homecoming game this Friday. Are you trying to run a few plays with me? I really gotta get'em down packed." Choyce just stood there in a blank stare.

"Lil' bruh, my bad, I got a lot on my mind right now. I'd love to, but I got something else going on, that I need your help with tonight," he replied.

I knew he wasn't going to turn back on his mission. He was hell bent to serve justice for Justin, no matter how hard I tried to talk him out of it.

So, I put all my fears to the side just to let him know, out of everyone on this earth, I was one person that he always could depend on.

"What's the move?" I stammered and looked at the ground.

"Let's go home, I'll tell you talk to you there." He then put his arm around my shoulder, and we walked towards the house.

We walked in, and Dad was still on the couch,

where he'd been for the last month. Mom let him do his probation from the house. He did all he could to find a job, but those felonies missed him up.

He gave up on life, and mom wanted nothing to do with him. He'd tried to right his wrong ever since he'd been home, but the scars that he left on our hearts, were too many to heal in just a couple of years.

"How was school?" he questioned. Choyce and I just walked upstairs without saying a word. We then went straight to Choyce's room.

"Look, Chance, I found out who the nigga was that killed Justin, and tonight, you and I are about to go rob him, and Unk will handle the rest," Choyce explained as we walked over to his closet. He pulled out two large black duffle bags, then tossed them on his bed.

"From what I was told we'll be straight, as long as we get in and out. Unk said it's a window at the front of dude's house, that we're going to climb in. It should be big enough for us and these bags to fit in," Choyce continued.

He walked over to his sock drawer, then pulled

out two wool ski masks and two pair of black leather gloves. He then walked back to his closet and laid us out two black hoodies and two pair of black jeans next to the bags.

"It's a safe in that room. Once we're in, we'll just fill the bags up quickly. So, we can get fuck back there," he commanded.

I stood stiff in the middle of his room, silent as my mind had begun to fill with all kinds of worst-case scenarios. He then stood in front of me, grabbed me by my shoulders, and looked me eye to eye.

"Look, Chance, you said you had my back. So, I need to know now. Is you wit this shit or not?" he questioned. My silence lasted for a couple more seconds.

I didn't like who Choyce had become, but something in my heart wouldn't allow me to let him travel down that dark path alone. I had to be his beacon of light somehow, someway. So, if he ever came to his senses, I would be the one to help him find his way back. Even if it meant helping in situations such as.

"I got you, bro, let's do this for Justin."

*****

9:45 p.m.

Justin's uncle picked Choyce and I up, a few
blocks down from our house. He told us to get in the back
seat and sit low. We rode for three more blocks and ended
up in an ally, before we stopped.

"I'm about to drop you two off right here then
park by his garage," Justin's uncle informed as he looked
around, to make sure no one saw us. Choyce couldn't
help but to notice that the house looked familiar.

"Aye, isn't this, Big Rick's house?" he asked. I
knew something wasn't right when he sat up with an
angered look on his face.

"This is the dude me and Justin used to buy
from. He put us on, and I know ain't have nothing to do
with this shit. So, the fuck is we here for?" Choyce
questioned again. Only that time, he pulled out a gun and
cocked.

My heart skipped a beat because I never knew
Choyce had a gun. Plus, I was saddened because I'd

never known Choyce to be a violent person.

"Choyce, clam down and pay attention! Big Rick is the one who sent those other nigga's to y'all! If it wasn't for him, Justin would still be alive, and we wouldn't be here!" Justin's uncle answered aggressively. He reached under his seat, then pulled out a gun of his own. After he cocked it, he laid it on his lap.

"Now, stand by that tree over there. When you see that light in the back room come on, I want you to creep low to that side window by the front porch, climb in, and clear the safe out," he demanded. I could tell by the way Choyce looked over at me, he felt like he'd been deceived but still went on with it.

"Once you fill those bags up, come back to the car, and lay on them until I'm done," he continued as he got out, then went towards the house. Once he was in, we made our move.

"Come on, lil' bruh, this niggah got us fucked up," Choyce said. We got out then stood by the tree.

It was cold outside, when I looked at the sky. Dark clouds covered the stars and moon, which gave them a hazed glair. I was so nervous my knees shook. Sweat dripped from my forehead, and my heart pounded heavily as I pulled my ski mask over my face. I pulled my gloves, so they fitted all the way on my hands, then stood close behind Choyce as he looked towards the house.

"Come on, Chance, it's time." Choyce commanded, when he saw the light came on, then pulled his ski mask over his face. We did just as Justin's uncle told us. We crept on side of house, opened the window, and went right in.

"Here it is, right here, lil' bruh," Choyce whispered as he referred to the safe. A soon as he opened it, our jaws dropped.

"Oh shit, bro, look at this!" I yelled right before Choyce shushed me. I just never seen so many guns, much money, and big zip lock bags full of drugs in my life.

"Chance, you grab all the money, I got the rest," Choyce ordered. I shook my head yes, and we got to it.

After we emptied the safe, we threw our bags out the window, climbed back out, and made it back to the car.

"Stay right here, lil' bruh, I got to make this move right quick," Choyce said. He shut the car door, then ran down the alley towards our house. He had the bag with all the guns and drugs.

He left me with the money in the back seat. He was gone for like thirty minutes before he came back and opened the car door.

"Where did you go?" I questioned with concern.

"It's coo, just give me your bag." He took the bags then hurried to split the money up between the two of them before Justin's uncle came out. He zipped them up and put them on the floor then hopped in with me.

We ducked down to play it off, like we did exactly what Unk had told us to do. It was an hour later, and he had just come back to the car.

"Did you kill him?" Choyce questioned and looked around as if he were scared.

"That nigga's a done deal," Justin's uncle replied. He started the car, put it in reverse, then pulled off.

*****

We parked in Justin's backyard.

"You two make sure them bags are zipped, then give them to me," he ordered as he got out and opened our car door.

"And then what?" Choyce questioned as he cuffed the bag he had and hesitated to get out.

"Shiid, we about to count this money, nephew," Justin's uncle answered. I just didn't trust him because when he smiled, I got a con artist vibe from him.

"Say less, then," Choyce agreed. We both got out and put the money bags on the trunk. As soon as we unzipped them, Justin's uncle whistled aloud.

"This looks like way more than fifty grand in these bags, nephews," he stated. His eyes were wide open and glued to the money. I could see the twinkle of greed in them.

"This is a lot of money, Unk, I just still can't believe Big Rick, is the one who set us up like that though," Choyce commented. He then looked way from the money and up towards the sky. I picked up on his vibe the entire time. I felt that he didn't believe that

Justin's uncle had told the truth. He just used us as way to put some money in his greedy pockets.

"Are you sure he's dead?" Choyce questioned, then turned to look at him for conformation. I even looked at him myself. I wasn't street orientated at all, but even I could tell something wasn't right, by the way he stared at all the money on the trunk of his car before he answered.

"Yeah, nephew, I did my part. I can see that you did yours. All that left is for us to do is, divide our spoils. So, let's count this money," he assured. He put a cigarette between his lips, lit it up, rubbed his hands together, then grabbed a stack of money.

*****

Three hours later

"I just counted fifty thousand myself," Justin's uncle said. He had a surprised look on his face. When he saw Choyce and I, still had a large amount of money in front of us.

"I got like, twenty-three right here," Choyce said as he continued to thumb through the rest.

"I'm counting out fifteen plus the rest of this," I said. I was in disbelief, that I'd just counted out fifteen thousand dollars for the first time.

After the count, we had ninety-six thousand dollars, that was thirty-two thousand apiece. Choyce and I kept our money in one bag; we gave Justin's uncle other one and parted ways.

It was going on 1:30 a.m. and the window that Choyce used to climb in, on the nights he came in late, was locked.

"Fuck! Chance, go in through the front door. If dad or mom, ask you anything, tell them that you and I were going over your playbook at the park and lost track of time. When they ask where I am, tell them, I'll be home shortly. Unlock this window for me when the coast is clear."

I was nervous when I walked up on the front porch, considering what I had taken part in. I just knew mom and dad were going to be in the front room, waiting to chew my head off. I put my key in the lock as quietly as I could, then twisted the doorknob.

I opened the door, and all the lights were out. I looked in the living room and the glare from the T.V. allowed me to see my dad laid on the couch, fully dressed asleep as he snored heavily. Mom was nowhere in sight. So, I crept to the side window to let Choyce in.

"Come on, bro," I said quietly as I opened it.

"What did they say?" he questioned as he handed me the bag.

"Dad's sleep and mom must be in her room," I answered. I sat the bag to the side and helped him climb in.

Once we made it to Choyce's room, I turned the light on and closed the door. I had to have a real heart to heart with him, and that was the perfect time.

"Look, bro. I know you said that you knew what you were doing, but I want you to know, I think your lifestyle is getting out of control. I worry about you, and I'm just scared that you're going to end up like Justin, bro. And if you did get killed or go to jail, then what? What will I do without you?" I said. I walked over leaned on his dresser. He was bent down in his closet as he pulled back a corner of the carpet.

"Chance, I already told you I got this. You don't have to fear the worst because it won't happen to me. I'm way different when it comes to the street life," he assured me, then walked over to his dresser to get a flat head screwdriver and walked back towards the closet.

"Besides, that's why I have this," he mentioned and stopped to pull out the gun from his waistline, then tossed it on his bed.

"Just so we won't ever get caught slipping again." He then walked in the closet and used the screwdriver to pull up the wooden floorboard.

"What about me? You're missing school, and I always walk alone now. What if someone tries to get to me because of something you did?" I questioned as I noticed Choyce drop the money bag in floor, put the wood flooring back in place, then cover it back with the carpet.

"Look, Chance. Justin and I made a promise to one another, that as soon as he reached one hundred bands, we would stop. So, I gotta keep that going until it happens. This is personal to me, once I get what I want, then I'm out," Choyce explained as he put his gun under his mattress.

"Well, if that's the case, you can keep all the money from tonight. I don't want any of it. But you gotta come back to school, so you can graduate, bro. I just don't see this as a promising future for you. Deal?" I questioned as I extended my hand to do our handshake.

"Deal, lil' bruh. Go get some rest. We gotta get up in a couple of hours," he agreed as we shook up, and I left his room.

*****

In school, I was sleepy and could barely hold my head up in class. A lot had changed in my life. I was eighteen and becoming a man. I had a light goatee and wavy hair. The way my muscles had developed, they complimented my dark skin. I was always fresh to death with a very bright future. The ladies started throwing themselves at me, and I wanted nothing to do with them.

"I see someone's been up all night studying," I heard Channy whisper as her soft lips pressed against my

63

ear.

"Damn, shorty, what you do that for? That felt good as fuck," I questioned as I sat up and placed my hand on my ear.

She just looked back and smiled at me. I couldn't help but to stare at her lips until she turned around as she walked to the front of the classroom and took a seat. I'd always saw how beautiful and full they were, but I never knew they were so soft.

She looked back at me again and smiled, my eyes got big, and I started to get an erection. I wasn't the only one that had gone through some changes over the years.

"Geesh," I said under my breath. When realized that not only had I just noticed her lips, but the rest of her body had gotten thick too.

After class, I hurried to greet her in the hallway. Out of all the years that I'd known her, that one moment we just had made me think about the time she had gotten into that relationship. I just couldn't see her with nobody else, if it wasn't me from that point forward.

"Damn, Channy, the fuck you got going on nowadays? I mean, that outfit you got on has your body looking amazing," I questioned as soon as she walked out the classroom, and I pulled her to the side.

"You like it? I made it last night," she answered and spun around to model it for me.

"Yo! That's dope, you got a real gift," I answered, enthused to show my sincerest support. She'd always made her own clothes, but her talent had taken off in a completely different direction.

"And guess what, though, this is the best part," she said as she stopped her spin directly in front of my face.

"What's good, shorty?" I questioned as I licked my lips.

When I looked at her, it seemed as if I had gotten frozen in time. She had on long eye lashes that complimented her beautiful, chestnut brown eyes. She had her hair in a curly hairstyle that was shoulder length. Her makeup was on point and all.

"I did this all, for you." She leaned forward and

kissed my lips. I felt a sensation go through my body that caused me to get hard again. I looked down at it then back at her. I was embarrassed because that was the first time that happened to me. It was like he had a mind of his own. Channy saw it and blushed.

"Well, Chance, I see someone's happy. You'd better cover him up, I'd hate to have to beat ah bitch ass today. I put in too much work, to prepare for this moment," she mentioned as she turned to walk away.

"And oh, give me your phone and the passcode, nigga. I would hate for you, not to be the one calling me, at this point in my life. Cause you know what they say? If you snooze, you lose." I was speechless as I reached in my pocket and gave it to her.

"2323, and save it under Juicy," I joked.

She smiled from ear to ear as she unlocked it. She then scrolled through my call log, then text messages.

"Boy, please I'm saved under Wifey. So, anytime you see that I'm on your line, you'd better answer. And this is an XR too. Oh yeah, let me go ahead share your location to my phone asap."

"Well, since we're making moves like this, you know the senior prom is coming up. So, would you like to go?" I questioned as I pretend to be cocky, but the beads of sweat that formed on my forehead gave me away.

"We'll see, you know y'all niggas ain't shit," she answered, gave me my phone back, then walked away.

I was confused like, what just happened? I wanted to chase after her, but I couldn't be late for my next class. One thing was for sure though; her impression was most defiantly felt that day.

Chapter 4

It was the beginning of spring and Choyce had me very impressed. Not only was he coming to school, he was passing all his classes. Although, he was still in the streets. He moved smooth with his business and kept a low profile. I saw what he meant when he said, he was different.

I had stopped worrying so much about his lifestyle because he knew what he was doing. Like I said, he was just an old soul that stayed twenty steps ahead of life, very rare and unique.

"Aye, lil' bruh, come here right quick!" he yelled and motioned for me, to come over to his locker. He had three other people lined by it. So, I made my way to the front.

"What's good, bro?" I questioned as we shook up.

"Meet me at your locker after school. I want you to walk with me on our way home. I got something that I want to show you," he explained. The look in his eyes made me want to question what it was about.

I just hoped he wasn't trying to involve me in any of his illegal activities.

*****

After school was over, I met with him at my locker like he'd asked, then we headed home.

"Bro, why are we going this way? It's bringing back bad memories," I questioned. When I noticed that we were headed the same direction, we took the day Justin had gotten killed.

"I can't help it, lil' bruh, this way means something to me. It's like I can still feel his presence. Plus, this is where I hide my stash now," he answered as he led the way. We ended up cutting through the same mini junkyard, behind the car garage we'd stopped behind on that day.

"Wait right here, lil' bruh," he said. I watched him as he took off his backpack and cut between a few junked cars. He stooped down for like three minutes, then stood up and put his backpack on.

"Follow me, lil' bruh." We walked south up the

alley and passed our house up.

"Chance, by the time you go off to college, I'ma have this city taken over," Choyce boasted as he walked with his head held so high that his chin could've touched the clouds.

"Bro, how long do you really think this lifestyle is going to last?" I questioned. He just looked at me with a promising smile on his face.

"Don't worry, lil' bruh, I won't make this my lifelong goal. I'll just keep it going long enough until you make it to the league. Then I'm done, you have my word," he assured. We got to the end of the ally, then crossed over to the thirty-third hundred block of our neighborhood.

We walked through a backyard just a few houses off the corner, then Choyce knocked on a back door.

"Who is it!" some older lady yelled.

"Who you think it is?" Choyce answered with authority, she then opened the door. She had a half-smoked blunt between her lips, her robe was half-opened, and her hair was all over her head.

"Oh, it's you. Come in," she said as she hurried to adjust herself.

"I see you bought company," she addressed as we walked in, she locked the door behind us.

"Yeah, this is my lil' bruh. Bruh, this is Justin's auntie, Unk's wife," he introduced.

"Nice to meet you," I said as I took a seat at the kitchen table.

"My, my, myyy, the apple doesn't fall to far from the tree, sometimes in pairs. You two are some handsome young men. Twins, I never had them, I gotta get some new walls," she said and did a little shimmy.

"Shut the fuck up," Choyce said as he fell out laughing. I had to laugh too; that was unexpected.

"Are you here alone?" Choyce questioned as he pulled himself off the ground sat in a chair and looked around.

"Yeah, baby, it's just me," she replied and seemed to have gotten anxious out of nowhere.

"You haven't told Unk what we have going on,

have you?" he asked as he looked up at her and placed his hand on his backpack.

"No sir, I told you, he's still fucked up in the head about how he gambled away all that money he had, in a week. The last thing he needs, is to find out I'm cooking your drugs for you.

"Good, let's get to it then," he said as he put his backpack on the kitchen table then unzipped it. He pulled a bag zip lock bag of coke out then handed it to Auntie.

"That's nine ounces, auntie, and I'm weighing my shit out when you're done."

She walked over to the stove and turned it on, reached in her cabinet, got out a soup pot, put some water in it, and put the pot on the stove. She then grabbed a big jar from out of her dish rack and used the bottom of it to crush up the coke.

Once it turned into a powder form, she poured it into the jar and added some baking soda. Once the water was at a boil, she then placed the jar in.

A couple hours had passed when she finished with the ninth ounce. She already had a long baking sheet, with the other eight laid on top of a few paper towels. Auntie dumped the last batch out on it then pushed it in front of Choyce.

"Weigh it, bag it, I don't give a fuck. Just give me my shit and, hurry up before that fool gets here," she demanded as she held her hand out and begun to tap her foot.

"Good looking out, Auntie. Here, make sure you hide this shit though. If that mufuckah find it, all hell will break loose.

"I'm not worried about him, but do you have any grown man?" Auntie asked. Choyce pulled out a zip lock bag full of brown powder.

"Yelp, here it is. You know, I don't like it when you do this shit though. Don't you?" Choyce questioned then poured some out on the table.

"I know, but this is for your uncle. I know, he didn't score, so I don't need to go through none of his shit tonight," she said as she left the kitchen. I was quiet the entire time, but as soon as she left, I questioned the hell out of bro.

"What's the difference between the white powder and the brown?" I said as he packaged everything up.

"The brown is heroin, but the streets call it grown man, dog food, or boy. The white is coke, but when it's cooked, we call it hard. You get it now?" he answered as weighed out his nine ounces and bagged them individually, so we could leave.

"Yeah, I got it, bro, just be careful and move smooth with this shit. At least until I make to the league, and I got you. We can leave all this stuff behind us."

*****

I was going to go home, but I decided to stay out with Choyce. I just felt more comfortable around him, since I had gotten a chance to see what he was into. He made money like crazy and all his transactions went smoothy. I was right there to witness.

Nobody tried to rob him. He didn't have to pull out any guns, and I could tell he had much respect on the streets. I took it as, it was in our blood to shine, in whatever we put our hands on.

"Let's go home, lil' bruh, I sold out for the day," he said as we walked back to bro's stash spot at the mini junkyard.

"Bet, oh shit!" I yelled. I looked down at my phone and noticed it was twelve a.m.

"Damn, you right. I lost track of time, this shit can get addictive. My bad, lil' bruh. I hope nobody's up like the last time," Choyce said as he hurried to swap out his money for his schoolbooks.

We thought everyone would've been sleep, but as soon as we stepped foot in the door, I heard dad and mom in an agreement upstairs.

"Why are you steady going at with him if I'm home? Huh? Your supposed to be my wife!" he yelled as Choyce and I stood at the door.

"I don't have to answer to you, and if you don't like what's going on, just sign the papers," mom replied in a calm manner. I could her, she'd gained her confidence back and wasn't about to allow my dad to make her act out of character.

"I'm not signing shit, you're mine! I don't

want my woman out here dressing like one of these young hoes! I don't want my woman dressing like no stripper!" he addressed in a demanding tone.

"Well, you must want a man then!" mom yelled back in response. I then slammed the front door.

"What, okay, you talking back now? Hold that thought," Dad said, and I could hear his heavy feet as they walked from mom's room towards the stairs.

"And I don't know who these niggas think they are, coming in all late and shit," he mumbled as he came down the stairs.

"Where in the fuck have you two been!" my dad yelled as he grabbed Choyce by the collar of his shirt and mean-mugged me.

"Man! If you don't get yo bitch ass hands off me!" Choice yelled and shoved him away, then gave him a vicious stare down. He lost his balance, fell backwards over a coffee table, and shattered a lamp. Before he could stand back up, Choyce and I stood side by side as we anticipated his next move.

"Oh, so, I guess I'm supposed to be scared now.

You two got a little hair on your nuts and think you're grown? Huh?" he questioned as he stood to his feet, then took a fighting stance.

"What's going on down here!" mom yelled as she ran downstairs.

"Your sons act like it's ok to come in all hours of the night! And as soon as I checked them for it, they acted like they wanted to jump me in my house!" dad explained as if he still had a say so.

"Your house? Clarence, look around, this isn't the same house that you abandoned a couple years ago. This is my house! I let you stay here because I felt sorry for you. That's it, you don't run nothing," mom stressed as she adjusted her nightgown.

"Well, I think it's time I reinforce some sort of order around here. Seems y'all forgot who the hell I am!" he yelled, but the fear that we once had for him was gone, we didn't budge and weren't worried.

"Nah, see, that's not about to happen. We've come to far as a family to stand by and let you slip back into your old ways. Things have changed, old man, and we're tired of your bullshit," Choyce replied. Mom didn't say a word; she just stood next to us.

"Oh, so it's cool to let them cuss in front you now. Never mind, I get it, you too busy sucking your new fancy lawyer boyfriend's dick, than to worry about the order of this house!" he said as he faced my mom like she was a target.

"Nah, you're not about to question her about nothing she has going on. We're the men of this house now, you abused your privileges. Really, if you don't like what's going on, you can get the fuck out," I said, and everyone looked at me with shocked expressions.

It was the first time I stood up to him. As I said, all the fear I had for him as child was no longer there. He was no longer a monster in my eyes, just a sorry excuse for a parent.

"Okay, if this is how it's going to be, I'm gone. I see want's going on," dad said as he walked out the house. Choyce unzipped his back and quickly threw something at his feet before mom could see what it was.

"This should keep you busy, for a while," he

said then slammed the door in his face. We never saw him again.

*****

Two weeks later

"How do I look, lil' bruh?" Choyce questioned as we got fitted for our cap and gowns.

"Like a true scholar," I answered while I checked myself out in the mirror. I was just glad to see my brother had pulled through, after all he had gotten himself into.

"I'm about to cut out, lil' bruh. I gotta go make sure that your graduation gift is ready. So, come straight home, and I got you," Choyce explained after he placed his order for his class ring and yearbook.

"Ok, bet. I gotta go holler at Coach right quick, he said it's urgent. After I see what that's about, I'll be on my way," I replied.

Being that we were seniors, we only had half-days, so I saw no harm in leaving school a little early. Once I got down to Coach's office, he and the entire coaching staff were waiting for me.

"Mr. Coleman, come in. Have a seat," he invited with a welcoming smile.

"What's good, Mr. Whitmore, am I in trouble?" I questioned, seeing everyone just sitting around made me nervous.

"Not at all, Chance, in fact, we're all proud of you. I called you down because the University of Alabama accepted your application and have offered you a full ride. So, congratulations." I couldn't believe it, that was where I wanted to go ever since I was a kid.

"Yo! Are you kidding me?" I questioned, enthused as I jumped out my seat.

"No, sir. You earned it, kid. They were impressed with your all-around talent on the football field and off. Your SAT scores were sky high, and they hurried to make sure I talked to you. So, you're officially accepted, your letter should already be in your mailbox today," Coach continued to say.

"Man, yes, I'm accepted!" I was so hyped that I couldn't stand still. That was the moment of a lifetime, and part of my dream had finally come true.

"Hold on, Chance, there's more. They also invited you to play in an all star game in Australia two weeks from now, so congratulations once again."

After I shook everyone's hand and thanked them for all they'd done, I left Coach's office on a high, I'd never felt in my life. I saw Channy as she walked down the hallway, so I had to share the good news with her.

We'd been communicating on the phone a lot and spent a lot of time together. We decided to take our time with another. We didn't want to rush anything because of the strong bond we had as friends.

"Aye, shorty, what's good!" I yelled as I ran up on her.

"Hey, Chance," she replied. I waited until I got close enough and swept her off her feet.

"Oh, okay, what's this about?" she said after I spun her around then set her back down.

"I'm going to the University of Alabama!" I rejoiced as I still had my hands around her waist.

"That's great, babe! You always said you

wanted to go there, now look at you!" she congratulated me as she wrapped her arms around my shoulders. I expected a hug, but she kissed me instead.

"Hey, I thought we said, we were going to take our time?" I questioned and took a step back.

"Chance, time is taking too long, and tomorrow isn't promised. You are who I want, and I know you want me to, so let's just see where this goes from here." As I looked into her eyes, I saw a spark in them, I'd never seen before. I just felt like I wanted to spend the rest of my life with her.

We kissed again, but it was slower and more passionate. I almost forgot where we were.

"Hold on, shorty, are you sure you really wanna do this with me? We've been friends for so long, that I don't want to take this step. If it's only going to ruin everything, we worked so hard to build with one another," I questioned as I held her close and looked into her eyes. She was way shorter than me but fit in my arms like the missing piece to my puzzle.

"Yes, I'm sure, Chance. I have just grown so

attached to you, that I want you in my life so badly."

"Okay, then we're official now. I got to go see my bro, so I gotta leave. Call me when you get home; we can finish talking there," I said as I let go of my hug and was about to walk away.

"Wait, you're about to leave the building?" she asked but had a concerned look in her eyes.

"Yeah, but I'll be back tomorrow, it's coo. I'll be okay." I turned and headed down the hallway towards the exit, and Channy yelled for me.

"Chance!" When I stopped to turn around, she'd already walked towards me.

"What's good, shorty?" I questioned.

"I'm going with you," she said and grabbed my arm, which left me no room to say no.

As we walked out the building, the sun hit perfectly. The sky was filled with white clouds, and a steady but gentle breeze surrounded Channy and I as we held hands and walked to go meet up with Choyce.

"So, sir, our prom is coming up. Have you planned out our night? Or should I go ahead and do it myself?" Channy questioned then leaned her head on my shoulder.

"Nah, I got it you, just make sure you match my fly, and I'll make sure it will be a night you won't ever forget," I assured.

"Speaking of fly, I see you came up with yet another bomb ass outfit," I gave my compliment as I noticed she had on a nice romper that hugged her curves perfectly.

"You know I make it do what it do," she boasted and pretended to pop her collar as we turned onto my block.

I noticed a red Hellcat drive pass then it slowed down. It went up a few driveways and turned around. It had dark tents all the way around, so I couldn't see in it.

"Chance, do you know who this is?" Channy questioned as she grabbed ahold to my arm.

"Nah, probably Door Dash or Grub Hub," I joked. Right when we were about to continue walking, the driver's window rode down halfway.

"Is that him?" the driver questioned.

"Yeah, that's one of them," the passenger replied. My heart raced as I yanked loose from Channy's arm hold.

That's when the driver yelled, "Get that nigga!" The back doors on both sides opened and two dudes jumped out with Dracos.

"Chance! Chance! What's going on! Let's go!" Channy screamed.

"Channy! Run! Go now!" I demanded. She wanted to stay, but I pushed her, and she did as I said.

"What's going on?" I questioned the driver, and he just rolled his window back up.

"Shut up, you bitch ass nigga!" one of the gun holders said as he cocked and put it in my face.

"Yeah, there's no honor amongst thieves, your days of stealing are numbered!" the other addressed.

I was just lost all the way around, I hadn't stollen anything and couldn't believe that was happening to me.

"I think you got the wrong person. I play football," I explained and hoped it was a misunderstanding. It wasn't until the driver rolled his window all the way, and I saw Justin's uncle on the passenger side, badly beaten.

"Man! Are you sure this is one of them?" the driver yelled out with aggression.

"I'm sure, let's get this shit over with," he answered.

"Pop the trunk then!" the driver demanded. That's when the trunk popped, and that's all I could remember after I got knocked in the head.

*****

"Big Rick, I'm telling you, man. I didn't have nothing to do with this shit. That was all him and his brother, Choyce, doing," I heard Justin's uncle plea as I regained my consciousness.

I was in a room with duct tape around my ankles and wrist with a piece over my mouth. When I looked out the door, I saw Justin's uncle on his knees with a gun pointed at his head. He was surrounded by Big Rick and the two other guys that had jumped out on me.

"Nah! I heard you was at the ticket house

gambling heavy, around the time my shit came up missing! And you damn near told on yourself. You slick talking bitch!" Big Rick explained and nudged Justin's uncle's forehead hard with his finger.

"I even asked you where you got all that money from when you came to spend with me, and you said it was your insurance money. You lying, mufuckah! Aye, you two! Beat the truth out this nigga! Right mufuckin now!" Big Rick demanded with a heavy, deep voice.

They began to hit, kick, and toss him around the floor like he was a rag doll. As I watched, I just knew I was next, and I'd never felt a fear like that in my life.

"What do you want us to do, with this mufuckah in here, Big Rick?" I heard someone ask outside the door.

"I got that, lil' nigga. Y'all just go take care of that other business for me, right quick." Big Rick entered the room in a bossed-up, aggressive manner as he bent down in front of me and snatched the tape off my mouth.

"You see that bum ass nigga laid out right there?" he questioned as he pointed over towards Justin's uncle.

He was on the floor with his nose leaned to the side, both his eyes were covered with blood. His forehead was split open and his arm looked detached but still in its skin. He made awful noises like he was crying but couldn't breathe. I was speechless.

"I know you don't want to end up like him, do you?" he asked then looked me in my eyes. I just shook my head no.

"You don't look like the type to run in someone's trap spot and steal, but where I'm from, I can't be too quick to judge a book by its cover. So, tell me why you did it?" His presence was scary. The way he hovered over me, had me not knowing what to say.

"Sir, please!" I yelled. I wanted to tell him about my football career, but before I could, he reached down and slapped me so hard. Both my ears rung, and I cried immediately. Big Rick cocked his arm back to hit me again.

"Don't move, you fat fuck! You put your hands on my brother, and I'm ah murder yo bitch ass!" I heard

Choyce yell out. He was in the doorway with his gun pointed right at Big Rick.

"What the fuck did you just say, lil' mufuckah? Say that shit louder, I couldn't hear you!" Big Rick stood up from me and turned to face Choyce, then looked him eye to eye.

"I said, leave him alone before I pop you!" Choyce demanded as he held a steady aim.

"Oh, I thought that's what you said." Big Rick reached behind his back to grab his gun, but he was too fat. Bro pulled the trigger and hit him in his shoulder. It went in the front and out the back.

Big Rick bounced off the wall and landed on his stomach. Choyce hurried over to me and took the tape off.

"Stay right here and keep an eye on him. Here, hold this," he said as he pulled out another gun then handed it to me. He then walked over to Justin's uncle.

"Bitch ass nigga, you killed your own wife!" he said as he kicked him in his stomach.

"You set me and my brother up! You lied on

your nephew's grave! Now, look at you! You cold hearted, jealous, worthless piece of shit!" Choyce stood over him and pulled the trigger.

"Fuck you, greedy mufuckah!" he continued as he stood over him until he took his last breath.

I had completely taken my eyes off Big Rick, when I saw Choyce pull the trigger. Big Rick had enough time to grab his gun and had it pointed right at Choyce. When I looked down, I panicked.

"No!" I yelled, which made Big Rick nervous/ He pulled his trigger and missed Choyce. I then emptied the entire clip into him. I stood there as I shook out of control.

"Bro, give me your gun and come on!" Choyce demanded as we hurried to jump out a side window.

We ran down the street as fast as we could. I followed Choyce all the way to the mini junkyard. Choyce banged on the back door of the car garage part. Some man opened the door, Choyce gave him some money and the two guns that we'd just used. The man took them and closed the door, and we then ran home.

"Chance, hurry up and go into the bathroom take off your clothes, then hand them to me. I want you take a shower, and don't worry about what just happened, okay?" I just nodded my head yes.

As soon as I got in the shower, I was able to think more clearly.

"Man, fuck!" I yelled as I banged my fist against the wall. I looked down as the water went down the drain. I could see my future going right down with it. I cried as I banged the wall even harder.

Choyce had already changed his cloths while I was in the shower.

"Lil' bruh, calm down before you wake mom up!" he yelled as he busted in the bathroom and put my clothes in ah plastic bag with his.

"I'm about to go get rid of these, so pull yourself together!" he ordered as he left out and shut the door.

*****

It was an hour later, and I was terrified as I laid in my bed on my back. I'd just had to murder someone. I used my hands to cover my face, and all I could think about was football and how I worked so hard to get where I was. I hadn't even started the second part of my dream, and it was already in jeopardy.

"Can I come in?" I heard Choyce question. He didn't even let me respond; he just walked over and sat at the edge of my bed.

"Listen, lil' bruh, you're safe. You don't have to be scared. You're still alive and in your own room. That should let you know that shit went the way that it was supposed to go," he said as he leaned forward to pick up my football.

"That's not a good explanation, bro. I got kidnapped and could've lost my life, today. My entire football career could be over right now! So, enough with the bullshit and tell me exactly what happened?" I demanded as I quickly stood to my feet with a puzzled look.

"Man! Fuck! I know, lil' bruh!" Choyce yelled. He covered his face with his hands in frustration then laid back on my bed.

"Basically, Justin's uncle lied to us. I knew it, but I figured if he did his part like he said, he was going to do. I didn't have nothing to worry about. I was going to use the money and drugs as a steppingstone to get out the game," he explained as he sat back up then dropped his head in shame.

"After Unk went broke, he found out his wife was cooking up my drugs for me. He pressured her to tell him where I got them from. She told him I got more than money from that safe." As Choyce gave a better explanation, all I could think about was when Auntie told us how Justin's uncle gambled away all his money, a week after he had it.

"He took his anger out on her and killed her. He then went back to Big Rick to get in good with him. He told him everything, but he also told on himself, that's how he got fucked too." I shook my head in disbelief. Auntie was a cool woman and didn't deserve to die like that. I no longer felt sorry for Justin's uncle; he got what he had coming to him.

"So, how did you find me?" I questioned as I

sat back on my bed and looked over at Choyce.

"Oh, yeah," he said as he reached in his pocket and got out an XR, "give Channy her phone back." He then handed the phone to me. I just looked at it.

"How'd you end up with her phone?" I questioned as the thought of when I told her to run came back to my memory.

"While I was at the car garage with my mechanic, Muhammad, checking on your graduation present, I saw her running past screaming and crying," he said as he shook his head.

"I told her to come here and asked what was wrong. She told me what happened, and I panicked, I didn't know where to start looking for you. That's when she told me, she had your location in her phone." He grinned as if he saw an angel with his own two eyes.

"Me and Muhammed dropped her off. He then drove me to you, and you know the rest from there," he answered then put his arm around my shoulder, like a proud big brother.

"She the one, Chance, She's the one." I just

looked down at her phone and shook my head in
agreeance.

Chapter 5

Senior Prom Night

"Chance, honey, come downstairs and let me look at you!" my mom called out for me, but I was too busy checking myself out in her life-sized mirror. I had on a cold, money green suit with the shirt to match. The jacket had a nice gold trim that matched my vest and tie.

"Here I come. Who's that nigga? You that nigga!" I said as I licked my fingers to smooth out my eyebrows. Then, grabbed a bottle of Dior Sauvage cologne to spray on my neck and wrist.

Choyce came through for me with some money green Loui loafers that had gold spikes on them. He also bought me some clear lensed, gold framed Balenci's. I was fresh, and nobody had nothing on me.

"Are y'all ready to get a taste of America's favorite chocolate?" I questioned from the top of the stairs.

"Boy, come on, with your crazy self!" mom said with excitement. As soon as I was within eyesight, mom busted out in tears.

"Oh, my God! Son, you are so handsome!" she rejoiced, gave me a hug, then kissed all on my cheeks. I had a grin from ear to ear.

"Looking sharp, young man," Mr. McFarland commented as he patted me on the back.

"Thank you, sir," I replied then turned to shake his hand.

"Oh, baby, let me get these pictures, so you can get on with your evening." I posed as if it were for the cover of a magazine. I felt that smooth.

"Look at, lil' bro!" Choyce said as he walked in the front door. We immediately shook up; he then took a few steps back to check me out.

"Thanks, y'all, for real. You all just don't know what your support means to me," I said as I looked at everyone in the room. Their proud smiles spoke volumes to my heart.

"We'll, you're very welcome, sir. But this isn't it, we got something else for you waiting outside," mom said. When I walked out, they had rented me a 2019

G-Wagon.

"Yo! It's lit foo sho, foo sho now!" I said as I ran up on it then turned around to look at my family with my arm's in the air. That feeling was indescribable.

We all stood in front of it while taking our family pics, and it was then time for me to go pick up my queen. My family had other arrangements; Mr. McFarland had been spending a lot of time with Choyce. It seemed like Choyce listened to him, and I appreciated it. He had courtside tickets to a basketball game. So, he'd invited Choyce and my mom.

Channy and I were made aware of their plans, so we decided just to meet up at her house, so her family could send us off. Her and my mom stayed on the phone with each other, so I already knew she was going to send a bunch of pictures to my mom.

When I pulled up and hopped out, Channy was already outside. she looked beautiful. She told me she'd went all out on her dress, but when I saw it, I was star struck. It was money green, long, and covered her gold-colored heels. Her back was out, but it came down into a nice length train.

She had gold trim, but hers had a pearl sequence with it. She had her hair in a nice up-style to make sure people could see how her makeup perfectly matched everything she had on, pearls and all. Her family rushed to greet me. I felt the warm embrace from her people as they walked me over to her.

"Hey, handsome," Channy said as I approached close enough to get my hug.

"Babe, you look beautiful. You really go hard with your clothes, and I can't wait until your brand pops off. I love how you look in this dress." I couldn't take my eyes off her, that's how amazed I was.

"Thank you, love, I know you're going to be right there with me when it does. But for now, my people are waiting on us to snap these pics. So, uhm, yeah, this way please," she joked to snap me out of my daze.

We snapped our pics, she introduced me to her family, and we were on our way. When we pulled up, all eyes were on us from the time we walked in, and we were lit the entire night.

We danced to every song and took hundreds of pics. I had made reservation for two downtown at Ruth's Chris afterwards. My mom had booked us a room at the J.W. Marriott. She had already given my room key.

After we ate our meal, I drove down a little ways and parked on a bridge that overlooked the canal's waterfall. We got in the back seat and had a perfect view of the lighting, and we could hear the water clearly. With the sunroof back, Channy had her head laid on my shoulder as we looked up at the stars.

"Did you enjoy yourself?" I questioned and looked down to see her comfortably curled up on me with her bare feet on the seat.

"I loved it, Chance, you really went all out for us, tonight. You just don't know how much you mean to me," she answered and started to cry.

"What's wrong, love? This is a celebration, not a funeral," I joked, but she was blue, and I didn't know why. I thought the night was straight out a romance novel.

"You just don't know how hard I prayed the

day, you got kidnapped. I was so lost without you. I thought, I would never see you again. It was a fucked-up feeling because the first time, I had ever fallen in love with someone, that I knew loved me back, had got snatched right out of my life," she sobbed. All I could do was hold her tighter.

"Don't worry, I'm still here, babe. God heard your prayers, and I'm thankful you were there to help me. If it wasn't for you, then things could've gone a lot worse. But you saved my life. Let's just be thankful we've always had each other's backs since day one. And because of that, we're able to share moments like this together. Okay?" I questioned as I looked down at her tear-filled cheeks.

She was too beautiful to cry that night, so I had to comfort her to ease her mind. She just didn't realize the part she played in my life that day, and I had to let her know she was a hero in my eyes.

"Well, I got something to tell you," she sat up, wiped her eyes, and said.

"What's good, love?" I inquired then kissed

her forehead.

"I've been accepted to the University of Alabama as well. I decided to go there because of the day I thought, I lost you. I figured if I ever got the chance to be with you again, I wanted it to last forever. You're not mad, are you?" she questioned and looked me in my eyes. She didn't know that news was greater to me than when I found out, I was going.

"Mad for what, love? I truly to have the girl of my dreams that's about to attend the school of my dreams with me. That's more than enough to make the rest of our dreams come true. Let's go out and show this world what real love is all about," I assured as I opened the cooler and pulled out a bottle of champagne. I already had two glasses placed in the cup holder.

"Fuck it, we grown now, let's pop this bottle and toast to our dreams coming true together, babe," I suggested as I handed her a glass.

"Yes, babe, please pour me up. I thought you'd never ask," she said and laughed.

*****

After a we finished the bottle, we got out to walk the canal and reminisced as we held hands.

"Channy, do you remember the first day we met?" I questioned and looked over at her with a smile from ear to ear.

"How could I forget, you and Jaden almost got beat the fuck up for playing too much," she joked and punched me in my arm.

"How did I almost get beat up?" I laughed then held my arm as if it hurt.

"I was the one that lost my friend, trying to defend you," I said as I continued to get my laugh out.

*****

It was the first day of middle school as Jaden and I walked through the hallway into the cafeteria, so we could check the roster to see if we made the football team. It was a long line, so we discussed what role we'd play once we seen, we made it.

"Man! I'ma be the star running back this year, you had your shine all little league. Now, it's time to put on your big boy pants. That's is entirely different

style of football, and I don't think you ready for it,"
Jaden said.

He and I played on the same team ever since
Pop Warner. He was still mad at me because he lost a
bet, we made a year prior on who was going the win
MVP and take home the big trophy that came with.

"Yeah, well, you know how things go when you
try to compete with me. I would sure hate to hurt your
feelings again," I boasted as I unzipped my backpack and
pulled out my football. I tossed it in the air to catch it, but
he caught it instead.

"Yeah, you lucked up on that MVP bet, but if
I hadn't got hurt, we both know that was mine. But like I
said, not this year, bro. it's my time to shine," he
exaggerated with an attitude.

"Wait a minute, did I just hear you say you
got hurt?" I laughed as I snatched my football out of his
hands.

"Dude, you sprung your ankle, at home at
that. And you on sat out for one game. So, don't even try
it. Face it, bro, second stream is where you belong. Shine

with them because you do it better," I joked. Jaden stayed in his feelings when it came to football. I was just better and didn't see why he always wanted to compete with me.

"Man, whatever," he said as we finally made it to the roster sheet.

"See, bro, the proof is in the pudding. First string running back Chance, Coleman; second string, Jaden Brown." I laughed again, because I saw how hard he worked to outshine me during tryouts.

In my eyes, he was just as skilled as I was; he just didn't want to listen and couldn't accept, when coach tried to inform him on where we went wrong. That wasn't my fault, I just learned from his mistakes and did all I could to prefect my craft. That's what got my shine, but he didn't understand that.

"Man! I'm way better than you, dude," he stated with his fist balled up as if he wanted to fight.

"Oh, yeah? Well prove it then, go long," I said as I patted my football and got ready to throw it. For the life of me, I didn't know what I was thinking. The cafeteria was filled with other students.

Jaden took off running as he weaved through people. Once I thought, I saw a clear spot, I threw it. That's when he jumped caught the ball and landed on a table right in front of a group of girls. One fell off the table bench.

I hurried over to help Jaden up.

"I told you, bro! I'm better than you!" he yelled and spiked the football right next to the girl that had fallen, then kissed both his arms. I knew he was playing, but she didn't.

"Dang bro, you almost hit her with the ball," I said as I picked it up and was about to walk off.

"Man, fuck her," he said as he noticed his wild dive on the table got mustard all over his white shirt.

"Excuse me!" the girl said and hurried to stand to her feet.

"Did I just hear you say, fuck me? After you dove on our table like some wild animal, caused me to fall backwards, and threw a funk ass football at me!" she questioned as she looked herself over to make sure nothing spilled on her then back up at Jaden and me.

When I looked at her, I just saw this short,
skinny girl with single braids that she wore in a ponytail.
Her clothes looked like she had on two different outfits
with all kinds of loose thread that hung from them. I just
thought her parents couldn't afford to buy her new ones
and rushed to throw that together for her first day of
school. She had on some fresh new Jordan 1's that
matched it though.

"Yeah bro, chill out, you could at least
apologize. I mean, all of that did just happen," I
suggested, but like I said, Jaden was a hot head that
wouldn't listen to anyone.

"Why you taking up for her, I thought it was
bro's before hoes," he stated, but before I could answer,
the little girl snatched the football out my hand and threw
it so hard at Jaden's face, it made tears fly out his eyes.

"Oh. Yo! You should be the quarterback on my
team. That was a nice throw!" I joked, but she took it as
me being funny.

"Oh, so you got jokes. What, you want some of
this too?" she questioned and held up her tiny little fist

like she was ready to fight.

"Nah, shorty, calm down. That was a compliment," I said. By then, Jaden was in his feelings, once again. He tried to fight her, but I held him back. She was going off the whole time.

The entire lunchroom had us surrounded as they laughed at the way that little girl gave Jaden the business. We had to go to the principal's office. While Jaden was in the office telling his side of the story, I had the perfect opportunity to apologize. I liked the fact that Jaden wasn't a small dude, but she wasn't scared at all and ready to defend herself.

"Aye, I'm sorry about how things went today. I feel like it was my fault, but I never meant to throw that ball your way," I said as I looked over out her. She had her arms folded with a mean look on her face.

"Well, I don't see what sense it made to play football in the lunchroom, anyway. Boys," she said then turned her head away from me.

I couldn't help to ask, but her braids looked freshly done, her shoes were brand new, but her clothes looked weird. The suspense killed.

"Aye, shorty, if you don't mind me asking, why are you dressed like that? Are you poor or something?" I questioned. She just looked at me like I was being funny again.

"No, I'm not poor. I'm a fashion designer, I made this myself," she explained as she looked herself over once again.

"Well, if it's any consolation, it matches your shoes perfectly. I'm Chance, by the way," I said then walked over to extend my hand.

"Thanks, I'm Channy, it's nice to meet you."

We shook hands and had been close ever since.

*****

"Boy, I swear if you didn't apologize and I had gotten suspended that day, you just don't know. I had a cake baked for that ass," Channy stated as she pounded her fist to her hand, then busted out in a laugh.

"But what ever happened to that punk?" she questioned and bit down on her bottom lip like she wished he was about to walk up.

"I don't know, after middle school, he and his family moved out of town. I hadn't heard from him since," I answered. He was becoming an enemy of mine anyway; I was glad he'd moved away.

"No, babe. Do you remember when his sister, Big Niece, tried to check you about it the next day? And you stood tall on her overgrown ass too?" I asked and stopped to laugh. That day was hilarious.

"I'm weak as fuck right now! How can I forget," she answered and busted out laughing.

*****

It was the day after Channy had gotten into to it with Jaden. And ironically, Channy, Jaden's big sister, Niecy, and I all had gym class together. I was about to toss around the football with a couple other people when I heard a commotion that came from a large group of students that stood under a basketball goal.

I rushed over, pushed through the crowd, and all I saw was Big Niece and Channy squared up about to fight.

"Nah, you wanted to fight my brother, yesterday,

110

now pick on somebody your own size," Big Niece said. I laughed so hard, I couldn't stand up.

Not because of the fight, it was because Channy didn't give a fuck how small she was. She was ready to go hands up with anyone, who fucked with her. Plus, Big Niece twice her size.

"Nah, you ain't my size yet, but I promise if you put your hands on me, I'ma beat the shit out of you until you are. Try me if you want to," Channy responded and put her hands up. I could tell she had a big brother, a father, or something because she stood there like she knew how to throw them hands.

"What? I'm Big Niece! Don't nobody want no smoke with me. What's up!" she said and put her hands up too.

"This is too much talking, get down," Channy responded, and the way she anticipated Big Niece's next move, allowed me to see that savage, I'd spoken of in her.

"Come on and make a move before our teacher comes!" she urged Big Niece to swing as she moved from side to side.

Big Niece met her match that day, and she found herself the one that didn't want any smoke. Everyone around couldn't stop laughing as Big Niece just stood there in silence.

"Girl, whatever, you don't wanna do this with me," Big Niece stated as she turned to walk away, but it was too many people in front of her.

"Move!" she yelled out, embarrassed that Channy had pulled her card in front of the entire gym class, and she began to shove people out the way.

A couple days passed, and Big Niece came up to Channy and I as we sat at our lunch table. She slammed her books on it like she still wanted to fight.

"You ready now?" Channy questioned as she was about to get up, but it went way differently than I'd imagined.

"Nah, I just came to apologize to you about the other day. Jaden didn't tell me the entire story, and I'm sorry. I respect how you stood up to me. I never met somebody that had the heart to do so," she said then rolled her eyes and folded her arms in a feminine manner

as she waited on a response.

Niece wasn't ugly; she always dressed fresh than a bitch, smelled good, and her shoe game was stupid. I'm talking Jordan's, Airforce Ones, Air Maxes, all that. She was just too big to wear girl clothes, that's all.

"It's coo, I accept your apology. Now if you will excuse us, we were in the middle of a conversation," Channy replied in a rude manner. I could tell she still wanted to fight, but was willing to let it go, by the way she looked up and grinned at me.

"Okay, that's all I had to say, and by the way, that dress is cute, girl," Big Niece said as she turned to walk away.

"Thank you, did you want me to make you one too?" she replied.

From that day forth, they were friends and nobody messed with Channy if Big Niece was around.

*****

"I promise your little self, used to have me cracking up. You wouldn't back down from nobody," I said as we stopped at secluded spot on a bridge in front of the waterfall and leaned on the rail.

"Yeah, I'm a beast and they had me fucked up," Channy said as she did a little flex with her arms.

"Speaking of Big Niece, do you still talk to her? I know her and Jaden got separated in their parents' divorce," I questioned.

"Yep, we're still friends through Facebook. As a matter of fact, I just made her prom dress, and here's how she looks now," she said as she pulled out her phone to show me a photo.

"Wow, this is Big Niece?" I questioned in amazement. She'd lost a lot of weight and looked completely different.

"Yelp, but enough of memory lane, sir," she said as she walked up and gave me a kiss.

"How do you wanna finish this night out?" she questioned as she looked me in my eyes. We had connected on an intimate level; I could feel her erotic desires. I grabbed both sides of her face then kissed her passionately. I kissed the side of her neck, and she begun to moan.

"That's my spot, zaddy, stay right there. I'm getting wet, oh shit." I worked her neck a little longer as her body submitted to me. I cuffed her breast with my hand, and she cuffed my dick with hers.

"I want you so bad, babe." We kissed longer, and our desire to seduce one another grew stronger.

I cuffed her pussy with my hand and rotated her clit. She moaned even more.

"Wait, not here, let's go to the room," she suggested.

When I looked at her again, I felt something different. I felt like if we did have sex, that it might've ruined something. I had bigger plans for her, plus we were under the influence.

"Look, babe. I want this to happen, but if we have sex tonight, how would this affect us tomorrow?" I questioned out of sincerity. I knew about foreplay, but I had never had sex before. I always wanted it to be special. Prom night had its own significance, and I just wanted it to end perfectly with no regrets.

115

"I agree with you, Chance. I mean, I've made it this far before, but I never had sex either. I always told myself my first time must be just right and not rushed. I appreciate you stopping this before we went to far. I would've done it, but I wouldn't have been ready," she stated, then turned around and leaned back on me. I just wrapped my arms around her waist.

"You just don't know how much more that made me love you. I still wanna go to the room, but could you just hold me all night?"

"I got you, babe."

Chapter 6

One month later.

It was Memorial Day weekend, and for the last few weeks, I had been waking up at five o'clock every morning. I had reoccurring dreams of when I shot Big Rick. Sometimes, I was the one getting shot.

"Man! No!" I screamed, awakened by a gunshot that sounded like it went off right by my ear.

"I can't take this shit!" I yelled and covered my face with my pillow. I was taunted by thoughts of me getting locked up for the rest of my life, and my entire football career that I worked so hard to achieve was done in vain.

"Bro, man, what the fuck?" Choyce opened my bedroom door turned on the light and asked.

When I pulled my pillow off my face, he could see I was drenched in sweat. I had dark rings under my eyes from all the sleepless nights. I thought, I was going crazy.

"Bro, I can't do this shit anymore. I have too

much to look forward to, and I can't go to jail for the rest of my life. I only did it because dude had a gun pointed at you," I cried. I wasn't a street nigga. So, I didn't know how to deal with the pressure that came with being one.

"Just chill, lil' bruh, everything is going to be okay. Believe me, it was either our lives or theirs, and you did what you had to do," he said as he walked out my room. He then came back in with a cold washrag.

"Here, wipe your face. I'm telling you, we good. Look, I got something special for you. I wanted it to be your graduation present, but it wasn't ready. I got you today, though. It should help to take your mind off that shit for a while," Choyce assured as he turned my light back out and left.

After he shut the door, I laid in the pitch black with my eyes open because my mind didn't eat me up as much, when I was awake.

"I'm sorry, but you were going to kill my brother, and I didn't know what else to do," I said as I closed my eyes.

I woke up a few hours later, took my shower, got

dressed, and went downstairs. Choyce texted me to meet him at the car garage. I ate a bowl of cereal then headed his way.

"Aye, bro! Check us out!" Choyce yelled as he stood between two cars covered in tarps. When he and his mechanic, Muhammad, pulled them off, I saw a camouflaged red and black 2019 Demon and a camouflaged black and red 2019 Hellcat.

They both had the all-round dark tents and sat on Forgiato rims. The way the lights in the garage hit the cars, gave off an allusion as if they were covered with a sheet of glass. They were that wet.

"Damn, bro, these mufuckahs good hard than ah bitch!" I yelled in excitement as I walked closer towards them.

"Look, lil' bruh. I don't have no idea what the fuck he just told me, he did to'em. All I know is they paid for, but I'll let him explain again. Muhammad," Choyce explained as he opened the car doors then pointed to his mechanic.

When I looked inside the Hellcat, it had soft red

leather interior with black trim and stitching. The Demon had all-black soft leather with red stitching and trim.

"I mean, I already told Choyce all I had done to them, so long story short. When it comes to the motor, transmission, paint job, and music, nobody in the city's fucking wit y'all. What I didn't tell Choyce is I decided to make the paint job's flip colors in the sun. The least I could do, considering how much money he put into these bad boys." Muhammad announced with a proud grin.

"Most importantly, if anything goes wrong, just know that everything is covered through your insurance. So, enjoy, fellas," he said as he tossed us the remote keys.

"Oh, shit, bro! Thank you, man, for real! I don't know which car you had picked out, but I got to have this Demon straight up," I demanded as I rubbed my hands together.

I never told Choyce, but that was one of my dream cars I wanted to buy after I got drafted into the NFL.

"I'm already knowing, lil' bruh. Have at it." We got into our new rides and peeled out the garage. We raced through the city until we hit the highway. My dash had 220 on it, and I did the entire thing. We left traffic in our dust.

We made it back home and pulled into the back yard. I had already talked to Channy; she was having a barbeque at the park with her girls and invited Choyce and me out.

"Lil' bro, you were handling that mufuckah on the highway! We were on some straight NASCAR shit for real for real!" Choyce yelled as he got out his car, geeked up. I couldn't deny going that fast was an adrenaline rush, and I could feel why he was excited.

"Real shit, bro, I never felt so much horsepower in my life. Thank you, once again. But check this out, Channy is having a barbeque at the park and invited us out. Let's get fresh and go," I suggested for a quick getaway and to ease my mind a little more.

"Come on, let's go to the mall then, it's ah play, lil' bro," Choyce agreed.

*****

We pulled up to the mall and got out. The

only word that could describe how Choyce and I looked was impeccable.

"Let's go to Macy's, lil' bro," Choyce suggested, then led the way. As we made our way through the mall, girls pointed and stared as if we were celebrities.

"Oh, look they twins too!" a group of ladies yelled out.

"Big bro, thank you for showing me how to take my mind off that shit. Straight up, you just don't know what this means to me," I said as we walked into Macy's and headed towards the men's cologne.

"Man, I feel you, believe me. It took me long time to figure it out myself. Sometimes in life, we gotta do things we don't want to in order to survive. I don't know how else to explain it. It's just ah crazy world we live in," Choyce gave his brief explanation before he picked up a bottle of Chanel Bleu De cologne. Once he sprayed it on a test strip, he was lit.

"Off top, this is the one I don't even need to smell shit else," he said and held the strip up for me to smell.

"Nah, for real, I like it, but Channy put me on to this Creed Aventus, right here. This shit smell good as fuck, and I gotta have it." After I made my selection, we separated to pick out our fits. I went straight the Polo section.

I immediately picked out something fresh, so I went into the dressing room to try it on. I stepped out to see if I saw Choyce, so I could show him. That's when I noticed two dudes that looked familiar. I couldn't remember where I knew them from, but saw they were looking at Choyce.

"Look at this nigga," one of the dudes said as he pointed in bro's direction.

"Ain't that the nigga you fought a couple years back?" the other guy questioned.

That's when I realized it was Noah, the dude Choyce beat up, and one of other guys that was there that day.

"Yeah, that's that hard head, bitch ass nigga. I told him to stay out the hood trying to make money before I got locked up. But now that I'm back, I guess he has to learn the hard way," Noah said as he shook up with his guy.

"Yeah, guess he ain't learned his lesson after we killed his bitch ass partner," I heard dude say in regard to the day Justin got killed.

"Nah, for real. I swear, I think one of them bitch ass niggas snitched on me and O.G. and got us locked up for that shit. Luckily, O.G. took the case for me, and I only got three years, but they gave him twenty-five years with ah L."

"Oh, yeah, damn. I didn't know that shit, but I saw where they parked. Come on, let's go before they leave," Noah's guy commented then they both hurried towards the exit.

The mall was packed, and we were parked by the front entrance. Once I saw they left out the back, I hurried to put my clothes back on then alerted Choyce. I hoped they were parked far enough to buy us some time to get away.

"Listen, bro, I just saw the niggas that killed

Justin. They talking like they on some bullshit with us, so let's go," I suggested, but Choyce didn't budge.

"I saw them too, lil' bro and trust me, they don't want these problems," he commented then held up his shirt to show his gun.

"Bro, last time we ran from these niggas, Justin got killed. It's just me and you, now. So, what do you think would happen if we run again?" he questioned then resumed to pick out his fit. Once he found it, he threw it over his shoulder, then headed towards the dressing room.

"I ain't going out like that, lil' bro, and I'll give my last breath to make sure you don't either. We ain't about to let these fuck niggas ruin our day. So, once we done getting our shit, then we can go," he stated as he stepped in to change his clothes.

"Nah, for real, bro. You're right, we ain't did shit to them. At this point, it's either our lives or theirs, and it's time to learn to stop fuckin with us, straight up," I said then waited as Choyce tried on his fit.

"Off top, bro, this Rock Revival fit go hard

than a bitch!" Choyce said as he came out the dressing room. I agreed, and he changed back out.

After we paid for our clothes, we made one more stop at The Sunglass Hut and were ready to go. We walked outside and looked towards our cars. We saw it was two parked directly in front of them. Five people stood at the hood of the first car.

"Here these niggas go!" Noah said as he stood from the hood of the car and pushed through his guys.

"What's up, nigga!" he yelled, and he threw both his arms in the air as he aggressively walked towards us.

"Man, go on with all that bullshit, now's not the time. It's too many cameras and too many witnesses," Choyce said as we stopped and dropped our bags on the ground.

The day Justin got killed, I was younger minded, I'd been through some much shit since then. Fear was no longer a factor in my heart; I was ready for whatever. I knew what it felt like to be close to death and realized I had to face it one day, just not that one.

"Nah, fuck that! You thought since I was locked

up, it was coo to make moves in my hood. I'm home now! And I ain't having none of it! All that shit you got going on in the streets is dead, fuck nigga!" Noah yelled and was then face to face with us. All Noah's guys stood a few steps behind him while Choyce and I squared up, side by side.

"Nah, for real, we know where y'all lay your heads and all. Like he said, y'all dead out here from this day forward!" the one that stood with Noah in the mall, addressed.

I expected the other three niggas to start with their bullshit. But when I looked over Noah's shoulder, they weren't saying shit just and passed a blunt to one another.

"Y'all niggas got a lot of balls standing this close to me, after what y'all did to my bro! I don't even got no rap for you! I should pop one of you bitch ass niggas right now!" Choyce yelled as he pulled out his gun but held it close to his side, so only us and them knew it was out.

"Like I said though, it's too many cameras and

innocent bystanders to be on this gangsta shit. But we gone get to it, believe that. You niggas better stay prayed up," Choyce demanded. The way he snapped, had all them niggas on hush.

"All that, I'm dead shit! Nigga! Come to the hood with it. I'ma still be bustin moves all through that bitch, and I dare y'all try to stop me. Fuck y'all thought?" Hold this, Chance!" Choyce said as he passed me the gun then pulled out a stack of money.

"That's my hood, bitch!" he said cocked his arm back and smacked Noah in the face with it.

"Nigga," he took a step back and muttered. He looked up and nudged at Choyce like he wanted to make his move but upped and aimed right at his chest.

"Fall back, fuck boy. These ain't the type of problems you want wit us!" I said in an aggressive manner.

I felt my face bunch up, eyebrows squelch together, and my lips tighten up. I just felt angry that we were yet again, minding our own business. But the same niggahs that caused us problems in the past and killed someone, I knew, were back in our faces with the same bullshit. I was tired of it, and I just wanted them to go away for good. I wanted to pull the trigger so bad, but Choyce alerted me.

"Aye, Chance, put that up. The police just pulled into the parking lot, let's go!" I tucked it under my shirt. We then picked up our bags and attempted to make it to our cars, but the police pulled up from both directions.

"Is there a problem here?" an officer asked as he got out his car. We all just stood there. Until one of the three guys that didn't intervene spoke up.

"Nah, officer, we all went to high school together. It's been awhile, so we were catching up on lost times, that's all," he answered.

It was something about them three dudes, I couldn't put my finger on. They didn't seem to be on the same bullshit, Noah and his guy were on. Even though I still didn't trust them, that was odd.

"Well, where did all this money come from, and who's is it?" one of the other officers questioned then looked around.

"That's this bum ass nigga's shit," Choyce said as Noah picked it up and pocketed it.

"Since this was reported, I'm going to have to ask you all to leave. You gentlemen have a nice day," a third officer said as they walked back to their cars and got in.

"This ain't over!" Noah threatened as took a few steps backwards. Then turned to head towards his car.

"Come on, bro, these niggas didn't want no smoke," Choyce said as he put his arm around my shoulder, and we headed towards our cars.

*****

We pulled up in the backyard and got out laughing.

"Bro, did you see the look on that nigga's face when you smacked him with that money?" I said. I laughed so hard, I had to lean on the trunk of my car.

"Hell, yeah. And that nigga talkin bout he just got out, but was at the mall with no bags? Nigga, don't be mad at us because none your niggas blessed your hand when you touched down," Choyce said as he opened his backdoor and got his bags out.

"Let's get fresh bro, fuck them." About a month back, Choyce had met a jeweler, who was around our age from Jamaica, named Black. He in was in town from Miami to do Choyce's grill.

That was around time I was really stressed the fuck out. So, bro told me to ride with him. We pulled up to a jewelry store then went to a back room. Choyce sat in a chair and got his entire grill done with permanent platinum and baguette diamonds. Bro's shit was cold like Johnny Dang did it himself.

After Black finished, he told us, he was on his way back to Miami and would cut Choyce and I deals on the drip game. So, I had him customize me a pair of Cuban canary yellow diamond screw-in earrings. One iced out canary yellow and one white Cuban link diamond necklaces, one had the cross emblem, and the other a Jesus piece. I also got a top and bottom gold grill made. I didn't want perms like my bro, but I did make sure it had hundreds of diamonds in it.

I had to bless Channy with a pink diamond Cuban link choker necklace and matching bracelet. I was going to surprise her when I took her on a date, but decided to bless her when I pulled up at the barbeque.

I wasn't into wearing grills and jewelry so, once it came in the mail, I left it in the box. I just felt like switching up my style for the day. So, after I got dressed, I opened the box.

"Oh, shit! Bro, come here!" I yelled. I didn't mean to fret, but once I looked in the mirror, I looked and felt like a king.

Choyce rushed in my room with one shoe on. His shirt was halfway on and an AK 47 in his hand.

"What, bro! Who you see!" he questioned as he ran toward my window and looked out. My mirror was right next to it, so he thought I saw someone pull up.

"Nah, bro! Check me out," I said as I turned towards him. The sun hit off my chain so hard, I could see the diamonds dance on his face.

"Straight pressure, bro! I told you this was the move; you look like you already in the league," he boasted and turned to walk out my room.

"Ight, since you wanna up status like that I'ma put mine on too, then," he bragged then left to finish getting dressed.

Choyce's drip game had his mouth, arm, wrist, and neck lit. It made me wanna take mine off and let him do his thing for the day. Before we left, Choyce pulled me to the side in the kitchen.

"Chance, you gotta understand when we go out today, we're gonna be lookin like two walkin licks, straight up. Every jack boy in city is going to be on us. Here, take this," Choyce said as he handed me a Desert Eagle handgun. It was big as fuck, and I couldn't see my self able to conceal it on my person without anyone noticing. I just put it under my shirt anyway.

"While you were getting dressed, I already put the Draco in my backseat. It got ah hundred round clip on that bitch. Niggas think it's sweet when they see young, flashy niggahs on they shit so we gotta protect ourselves, lil' bro," Choyce explained as he looked me eye to eye.

"All we're trying to do is have fun today. If

ah mufuckah pull up on some dumb shit, we bout that, ASAP. Let's go fuck they heads up." We shook up and headed out the back door to our cars.

The feeling I had was surreal. I graduated high school, had a full ride scholarship to the school of my dreams, I had the girl of my dreams, and I felt unstoppable.

Once I got in the car, I tossed my gun on the passenger seat. I put my foot on the brake and push-started my Demon. The engine was so powerful, it roared loudly and made me feel infamous.

*****

We pulled up to the park, and it was so many people at the barbeque. It looked like a block party. Once we found our parking spots, we hopped out. We couldn't even make it out the car; all the ladies were on us.

I knew Channy was crazy as fuck over me; I couldn't see myself disrespecting her. I made my way through the crowd while Choyce stayed back on the smooth Casanova shit, he was known for.

I saw her by the DJ stand as she danced to

Megan Thee Stallion's song *Pull Up Late* with a cup in her hand. She had on biker shorts with a body suit I could tell she made. She was wearing yellow hoop earrings with some yellow Balenci shoes. Her back was towards me, so I crept up close behind her and started to dance.

"Whoa! Nigga, do I know you?" she sat her cup down turned around and said. I was in awe when I saw the front of her shirt was cut like a low V-neck that complimented the size of her boobs, and I could see her nipple piercings. When she saw it was me, her mouth dropped. My entire switch-up was to impress her. I was glad she liked it.

"Oh, yeah, you doin it like that, zaddy?" she said then turned around and started twerking on me.

I busted out laughing because although she was really twerking, I knew it was a part of her spontaneous sense of humor, plus she was a little tipsy.

'Nah, I'm just kidding, babe. But you know you're up here lookin fine as fuck and smell even better. Oh, and I'm loving the drip too," she said and gave me a hug. I had her gift in my hand behind my back.

"I'm glad you like the drip because, I got you a little something too," I said then presented it to her. Once she opened it, her eyes lit up.

"Thank you, zaddy! Aye, aye, aye, this my chocolate nigga right here! You hoe's ain't fuckin wit me! Cuz, peeriiiod!" she yelled out. She put one leg up on my side, her hand on my shoulder, and made her ass jump heavy as the DJ played a Megan and Moneybagg song.

I laughed harder because I know she was playing, but serious all in the same time. She was just crazy like that.

"Let me put it on you," I suggested as she handed me the box back.

Once I put it on, a loud group of females came and stood in front of us.

"Aye, this my shit," one of them said as she twerked to Megan's song *Savage*. I noticed one of them was on live and kept her phone on Channy and me.

"Hold on," she said as she looked at her screen then walked over to us.

"Do you sell loud?" she questioned

"Nah, bitch, he plays football," Channy responded before I could.

"Oh, okay, my bad," she said as she turned around looked at her phone and said, "Yelp, it's him.

"Fuck you mean that's him! You don't know him! Who invited you to my shit anyway?" Channy questioned as I held her back. I had a bad feeling and remembered my gun was in my car.

"Come on, babe, I gotta show you my new car, fuck them," I s suggested, then took her by the hand.

"Let's go because bitches is rude, and I like to fight," she answered as she mugged them bitches until they were out of sight.

"Oh, shit babe, it looks even better in person!" she rejoiced.

"Thank you, and it beat too," I said as I got in and turned on the music. I had *Coco* by Pop Smoke playing.

"Okay, I can't wait to flex this all over the city. You feel me," Channy said as she was about to turn up again.

She stood in front of me. I looked over her shoulder and noticed one of the black cars from the mall earlier that day, a few feet away.

The driver's window rolled down, and all I saw was a handgun with a long clip. Bullets and fire began to jump from it, and Channy let out a faint sound then fell forward and did a slight turn into my arms.

"Channy!" I yelled. I looked down and blood had begun to soak my shirt on my right side. She had gotten shot somewhere in her back and was unresponsive. Everything happened so quickly.

"Babe! Babe!" I yelled as I opened the back door and laid her across the seat.

Time wasn't on my side, I wanted to jump in and rush to the hospital, but something took over me. I reached over and grabbed my Desert Eagle, then took off running in the direction the car was headed.

"Chance! The fuck just happened?" Choyce questioned as he rushed to grab his Draco.

"Channy got shot!" I yelled as I aimed for the back windshield. I opened fire and shattered the glass, but the car kept going until it was out of sight.

"Fuck!" Choyce screamed because he had gotten there too late to fire at them with me.

"Come on, bro! We gotta get her to the hospital!" I demanded as I rushed back to my car.

"It's okay, babe!" I got you!" I assured Channy as I jumped in and pushed start to smash out.

"Get the fuck out the way!" I demanded and repeatedly blew my horn.

Once everyone moved out my way, I hit the gas. I did the entire dash as I weaved in and out of traffic and ran red lights. It took me seven minutes, and I was at the emergency room's front entrance.

"Help!" I yelled as I ran to open my back door.

"Channy! Can you hear me, babe?" I questioned, and when she didn't respond, I got nervous and thought she was going to die.

"Come on, bro, we gotta get her in here!" Choyce said as we got her out, took her inside the building, and laid her on a cushioned bench.

"Oh, my God, what happened to her?" a nurse questioned after she rushed over from behind her desk to check her pulse.

"She got shot in a drive-by!" I yelled out as I stood up and put my hands on the side my head. I was in disbelief. I couldn't believe my babe was shot; my head started to spin. I felt like I wanted about to pass out.

"She's been shot! She's still alive, but she's in shock," the nurse explained to the doctors as they came from the back with a stretcher.

"Ok, let's get her back for immediate surgery. It looks like the bullet went in through the back of her shoulder and lodged in her scapula," the doctor stated.

The doctors and nurses hurried to put her on the bed, then rushed her back to the operating room. I helplessly stood there as I watched her until the door closed.

I looked down at myself; my hands and clothes were covered in blood. The thoughts of every moment we'd ever shared quickly flashed through my mind, all the way up until I heard the gun shots and she fell into my arms.

"Bro, the police wanna talking to us," Choyce said as he put his hand on my shoulder

*****

When we got questioned, all we could say was Channy was shot in a drive-by. They had to let us go. I dropped the car back off at the garage and hopped in with Choyce.

"Somebody has to pay for this shit, bro!" I yelled, my emotions got the best of me. Tears filled my eyes, and I couldn't control my evil thoughts.

"We on that shit, lil' bruh, I got my people making calls right now. Let's go home, you get showered up, and change out. I need you to relax."

"Relax! Bro, these niggas is on some bullshit! They already took somebody from you! And just tired to take somebody from me! Bro, if she dies, I swear to God! I'm not going to stop killing until every last one of them bitches is dead! I want blood for my shorty!" I demanded.

I was done with the good guy shit. No matter

how different I tried to be, there was always going to be someone that hated on me, I was done. I needed revenge for my shorty before the sun went down.

Chapter 7

It was going on nine o'clock, and I still hadn't heard a word about the whereabouts of the nigga that shot Channy. I was sitting in my room as I thought over everything I had to lose.

It was sad when I realized the nature of my people. What was it that made us hate each other so much? How did we get so manipulated by foolishness that we'd kill each other to get it?

I looked down at my phone and hadn't realized it was on silent. I had three missed calls from Choyce.

"What's the word, bro?" I questioned as soon as he answered.

"Get dressed, I got they location," he replied.

I walked in his room and got dressed in all black. I got a gun from his hiding spot then cocked it.

"Chance, can I—" my mom attempted to say as she walked in on me with a gun in my hand.

When I looked at her, I was speechless as tears immediately filled her eyes. She put her hand over her mouth turned around and ran out the room. I tucked the gun under my shirt and went downstairs.

"Please, talk to them! I don't want them to get killed out here! Those are my babies!" I heard my mom cry out to Mr. McFarland, but I had no time to talk though.

I cut through the dining room and headed towards the back door.

"Aye, Chance, I heard about what happened today. I'm very sorry about it, but before you walk out that door, can I have a word with you?" Mr. McFarland asked as I had my hand on the doorknob.

"I don't have no rap right now. I'm about to go handle something, and I don't need you to try and stop me. You don't have to deal with struggles of being from around here. So, you can't relate to my pain. I gotta go," I replied. I knew Choyce was about to pull up, so I opened the door, but Mr. McFarland rushed over and slammed it back shut.

"The fuck is you doing, man! Get the fuck away from me!" I yelled and bucked up on him and looked him eye to eye. He was still in my way, so I shoved him.

"Aye! Calm down! I'm not your enemy!" he said as he grabbed the collar of my shirt and pinned me against the door.

"Don't hurt him!" mom yelled.

"Don't worry, I got this. Go in the living room," he said, then let me go.

"Look, I know all about these streets! I was one of the original gangsters that came from this same neighborhood!" he explained.

"I know all the pain that comes with being from the ghetto! I changed my ways when I witnessed my own brother, get his brains blown out right in front of me! My youngest brother is locked up and, won't ever see the day light again!" he said and took a step back.

"I lost my mother due to a drive-by, I lost my father because I sold him so muck crack, he overdosed. So, you don't know what pain is until you've seen it on my level." I didn't know what to say. All I knew was time was ticking, and I wasn't about to back down like no hoe.

"All I'm trying to tell you is, think before you act. Because due to my actions, I lost everyone, I ever loved. Now, I'm trying to redeem myself by being a lawyer. If you think what you're about to do is going to help you sleep better at night, then do what you gotta do. Just know that your mom and me, we want you to stay here. You're a grown man now, so the choice is yours."

I felt what he was saying, but it was going in one ear and out the other.

"Am I free to go?" I questioned and gestured at the doorknob.

"I'm not about to hold you up any longer, just know I have your back. I know you don't know me like that, but I love you. Hopefully, we'll get another chance to talk. But just know that we're here for you."

I made it outside noticed a black SUV parked in the alley. It was too dark to see in, so I pulled out my gun. The window rolled down, and I was about to take aim.

"Come on, bro!" Choyce yelled as he turned the interior light on, so I hustled to get in.

"What took you so long?" he questioned as he loaded an AK with a red bandana. I looked in his backseat, and he also had his favorite postal grip pump.

"Mom and Troy was on one and tried to convince me to stay," I said and laid my seat back.

"So, where's these niggas at?" I questioned as I pulled out the gun, I got from his room and laid it on my lap.

"They in the hood, right around the corner. I got one of my slimes over there right now, telling me they every move. Peep this though, he told me they'd been on bullshit all day," Choyce said as he got out to put his K in the back seat then got back in.

"He said they hit a lick on some niggas from out of town. They got about five bricks of coke in there with them right now, and they've been trapping hard all day. After we get at them, I need you to help me pack that shit up. You got me?" Choyce questioned as he looked over at me.

"Say less, bro," I said as I rested my head.

Choyce introduced me to his lifestyle, and he

wasn't a sloppy dude. I was in on the first lick he ever hit, I saw what he did with that, and I ended up in an up to date Demon. So, I was all for seeing him proceed to the next level.

After we circled the block a few times, we pulled in the backyard.

"Here, bro, put this mask on. I would say fuck it but, we can't afford no witnesses," he said as he handed it to me. Choyce sent a text to his guy on the inside.

"Fuck!" he yelled out.

"What?" I questioned as I looked around.

"That bitch ass nigga, Noah, just left. I circled the block too many times," he explained as he looked up towards the back door. His guy had just walked out then walked over to us.

"Yeah, man, that nigga just pulled off. I didn't hear where he said he was going, but the rest of them are still in there," he explained.

"What are they doing, bro?" Choyce questioned.

"In there high off them pills and lean. Them

niggas sleep on the couch like the three stooges and shit. I left the back door unlocked though." He informed that we had the green light then got in his car.

"What do we do if Noah's not in there?" I questioned Choyce.

"We still gotta go in there. We put that pressure on them, and they'll tell us where he is," he answered as we got out. Choyce got out his pump and handed me the K with the extended clip. I put the other gun under his seat.

We opened the back door then crept through the kitchen; all we could see was the glow from the TV in the front room. As we walked in, I saw the three dudes from the mall I had my suppositions about. Choyce's guy was right, they were high as fuck sleep on a couch in front of a long coffee table with thousands of dollars stacked perfectly on it.

"Wake the fuck up!" Choyce demanded as he let off a round from his pump in the ceiling.

"Don't move! Don't make a fuckin move!" I said as I noticed one of them reach for his gun. I had the K aimed at his head.

"Where's that bitch ass nigga, Noah, at?" Choyce questioned as he walked over to the person closest to him and put the pump on the tip of his nose.

"Aye, look! He ain't here, but I can take you to him right now. Just don't kill me," he pleaded. I wasn't buying none of it, so I started on my bullshit.

"Which one of y'all was with him when he shot my shorty?" I questioned as I waved the K back and forth.

"We ain't have nothing to do with none of that. Our O.G. sent us at that nigga for snitching on him. Noah lied on O.G. about a murder he did himself and got O.G. twenty-five to life. The reason he's still alive is because of the lick we hit today," one of three hurried to explain.

"Bro, he's telling the truth. He invited these niggas from New York to do business. We had this planned for a week, and after we were done counting this money, we were going to out him, but he left already. He's laid up right now in a room out north," someone else commented.

"I ain't buying none of this shit! You niggas

hurry up and start stuffing that money in bags by your feet, right mothafuckin now!" Choyce demanded in an aggressive tone.

They gave us dude's location, packed up all the money they made and what was left from them bricks. We then pulled our ski masks back.

"Please, don't kill us!" someone said with their hands in the air.

"Can we trust them, bro?" I questioned. If they didn't have nothing to do with it, I was against the spill of innocent blood.

"Nope, survivors always live to tell the story. Hurry up and get these bags out of here, lil' bruh, take the pump and give me that K. I got it from here," Choyce demanded. I got everything out the house and jumped in the driver's seat.

A few minutes later, one of the guys walked out the back door. I feared they overpowered bro and was coming for me next. So, I reached over and got the gun from under the seat.

That's when I noticed Choyce walk out behind

him with the K pointed at his back. He walked him over to the back door.

"Bruh, give him a bag," Choyce said. I got out, opened one of the bags took some money out, and handed it to the dude.

"I spared you nigga's because I believe y'all. Take that shit and disappear. Don't come back to the hood or it won't be ah next time," Choyce demanded in a stern tone.

"I got you, bro. We gone but kill that nigga, man. He's ah reckless rat," dude said as he took the money and went back in the house.

*****

It was two o'clock when we pulled up at the Motel 6 on the north side. We rode around the parking lot until we found his car. We then parked next to it.

"Bro, let me see if this fuck nigga left the receipt to his room, in his car right quick," Choyce suggested as he got out.

His doors were locked, but Choyce picked up

152

something up off the ground.

"Look bro, this is the paper with the room number the door key be in," Choyce said as he got back in.

"I hope it's his room. I don't got time to look for this nigga all night," I said as I looked around. The coast was clear, but we had no way to get in the building.

"Hold up, bro. I'm about to stand by this side door. Hopefully, someone comes out," I suggested.

"This personal, bro, so I'm only going to take this handgun. I just need you there to have my back," I continued as I got out.

I just felt like if we were able to get in, it was his time to go. I stood by the door with my head down, so the camera couldn't see my face. Forty-five minutes had passed, and no one came out to let me in, so I walked back to the car.

"Come on, bro, we'll just come back in the morning," I said and felt as if I had let Channy down.

"Just be patient, bro, I got a feeling he'll have

to come down to his car. We just have to play the waiting game," Choyce assured as he laid his seat back.

I was on high alert. Every time I saw someone come out the door, I clinched my gun and reached for the door handle.

Another hour had passed, and I just wanted to give up and let my seat back.

"Game time, lil' bruh. Let's get this nigga," Choyce patted me on my shoulder and said.

He was coming down the stairs, and we only had seconds to get out and position ourselves before he walked out the door. We pulled down our ski masks, got out, and ran to duck behind the SUV. We heard him in an argument on his phone.

"Bitch, fuck you! Did you want the drink or not?" he questioned.

Choyce and I saw that he was distracted and waited until he opened his car door. I pointed my gun as I ran around to his driver side and yelled, "What now, fuck nigga!"

When he turned my way, I pulled the trigger. It

went right through his cheek, and he flew backwards. He hit his car door and slid down to the ground. That's when his head fell forward.

"Come on, bro!" Choyce yelled.

I was stuck, I couldn't believe I did it. I started to shake. My feet felt like cement bricks.

"Bro!" Choyce yelled, then pulled me by my shoulder. I was so nervous that I fell, but I managed to get back up. We got in the SUV and peeled out the parking lot.

*****

I went to visit Channy; she was out of surgery and under sedation. When I walked into her room, I had to stop at the door. I hated to see her laid in a hospital bed with IV's in her, and it made me tear up.

"What's up, babe?" I questioned as I walked over and kissed her forehead.

I sat in the chair next to her bed, I couldn't help but to stare at her. I thought about the time when we were in the G Wagon after our prom. She cried because she thought she'd lost me when I got kidnaped in front of her. I could relate to her emotion.

I promised myself that I was going to put her ring on her finger as soon as she recovered.

"Don't worry, babe. I got'em for you," I said as I stood up and tucked her in. I got out an extra cover and reclined in my chair.

As I slept, my nightmares came back with a vengeance. I was haunted by the people whose lives I'd taken. I woke up in a cold sweat, and Channy's nurse had just came in the room. So, I let her do what her job, and I left to check on my brother.

I got home, and mom was on the couch sleep. I saw her cover on the floor, so I walked over and put it on her.

"Please, God, please," she said as she talked in her sleep. I just kissed her on her forehead and went upstairs.

"What's up, bro?" I questioned as I walked into Choyce's room and noticed he was on the phone.

I looked around his room, and he had stacks of blue hundreds on his dresser.

"Ight, bet, let me call you back though," he said as he turned to look at me.

"What's good, bro? How's Channy?" he asked as we shook up.

"She good, but I'm not, bro. I think, I'm really fucked up. This shit is haunting me, and I don't know how much longer I can hold on. I'm losing it, bro, and I don't know how I'm going to make it to college like this," I said as I looked him in the eyes.

"Lil' bruh, I'm sorry I ever introduced you to this shit, but don't give up on your dreams. Chance, you don't know half of the dark secrets people in the league hold within themselves," Choyce said as he sat on the edge of his bed.

"You and I saw on the news ourselves. The type of things players got themselves into off the field or court, in every sport. Don't get me wrong, I never in a million years pictured either one of us having to catch bodies behind the bullshit that we went through, but it happened, and there's no going back. You gotta stay strong because it's a reason why you had to do it. It's not your fault, lil' bruh. It was either us or them," Choyce said as he stood to put his money up.

He had a point. Sometimes, we had to make it out of our nightmares to live in our dreams. I not only thought about all the sports players that had gotten into trouble, I also thought about all the politicians, law enforcement, even presidents. It was clear that everyone on this earth had a little dirt under their fingernails.

"Listen. My slime, Black, the one with the jewelry, invited us up to Miami. We fly out in a week, mom's stressin the fuck out. Let's stay here for the next week, chop it up with her to ease her mind, catch our flight, and come back focused. I'll even train with you. Just don't go crazy on me, bro. I need you more than you'd ever know. I love you.," Choyce suggested as he gave me a hug.

I was all for it. The thought of flying over my problems and leaving them behind was much needed.

*****

Arriving at the airport

I caught a flight a couple months back when I

flew to Australia for my all-star game. I thought I saw the LYFT driver take the wrong exit for our terminal.

"Aye, we were supposed to make a left," I said, and Choyce just laughed.

"Chill, bro, we on something different," he said as the driver kept going.

When pulled up to a private jet, the driver stopped.

"Is this the one?" he questioned.

"Yeah, this us," Choyce said in a nonchalant manner. I was amazed that once again, he came through for me in my time of need. I'd never flown in a PJ before.

"Bro, we're kings, so I couldn't think of any other way to take our first trip as grown men than on a private jet," he said with a proud grin on his face.

"Off top, bro!" I yelled in excitement.

"Once again, thank you for being there for me. I be right on the edge, and you pull me back every time," I said as we hopped out and looked at the jet.

"Get used to it, bro, because when you make it to the NFL, I'm looking forward to the private trips overseas, on you," Choyce replied.

As we boarded the jet, it looked like we'd walked into a living room. It had a few flat screens, a soft black leather couch, and three exclusive black leather recliner chairs on each side of it. It had two more rows of regular seats. The back was lit; it had a bar and two office like settings on each side by the restroom.

I liked how the chairs had dark cherry red woodgrain footrests. I kicked off my shoes and adjusted my seat to lean back.

"We got champagne, bro, let's pop this bottle. We got a short flight, I just wanted us to enjoy the moment," Choyce said as he sat next to me with the bottle and two glasses.

After we finished the bottle, I finally had a chance to clear my mind.

"Bro, how you feel, now that we're finally getting away from the city for a minute?" Choyce said as he reclined his chair and kicked back next to me.

"It feels wonderful, bro, I'm just looking forward to having a good time and coming on back home, so I can focus on college." I laid my seat back some more and looked out of the window to soak it all in.

"Well, don't think about home too much. We'll have plenty of time focus on that when we get back. So, let's live in the moment," Choyce replied.

The captain told us we'd land in two hours and forty-five minutes, so I turned on the TV and watched my favorite movie *Carlito's Way*.

*****

Arriving in Orlando

On the flight, I had time to watch my favorite movie and think about my life. I had my plan together and as we exited the jet. I stopped to take in a deep breath, looked up towards the blue sky that was filled with white clouds, and exhaled.

I was relieved and felt innocent again. I embraced every step we took on that red carpet all the way to the SUV that awaited us.

"How you like the flight?" Choyce questioned as he drove from the airport.

"Peaceful, bro. I felt like a true boss," I replied.

"Good because we're here for the next two weeks. We got plenty of money, so we can go anywhere we wanna go," he assured.

It felt good to be away from all the stress of my city. I thought to myself once again as I looked out the window and saw willow and palm trees everywhere.

"We're going to our resort home here in Orlando. After we get ready, we'll hit up the mall then Daytona Beach. It's about an hour from us," Choyce explained as we went through the city. It was a beautiful place.

We pulled into the garage of the resort home then walked in. It was nice four-bedroom with a bath in each room. It also had a pool table and upstairs living room. The back patio had a fenced in heated pool with a jacuzzi. The only reason for the fence was to keep the alligators out.

*****

Daytona Beach

After we hit up the mall, we pulled up to Sea

Breeze Drive. Once we parked, we found a place to change into our swim trunks, then put our clothes back in the SUV. We were ready and headed for the beach.

"Fuck, lil' bruh, it's super hot out here, the fuck it this about? It was just raining," Choyce complained about the weather.

"Off top, bro. Since we'd been here, it's rained, got cool, the sun come out, then rained again," I joked in agreement.

We walked for a few blocks until we got to the beach. As soon as my toes touched the sand, I saw nothing but the strong waves of the turquoise blue Atlantic Ocean.

"This is what the fuck I'm talking about, bro. let's go cool the fuck off!" I suggested as I took off running towards it.

I didn't hesitate, I just jumped right in. I hadn't been swimming since Choyce and I were in middle school. I swam in the ocean as if the saltwater could cleanse me of my sins. I got out the water, and Choyce had us two chairs.

"I saw you in that water like Mike Phelps," he said as he threw me a towel.

"I needed that, bro, for real. That shit got my mind so clear right now," I replied as I dried off and sat next to him.

"So, what's the play for tonight?" I questioned.

"As a matter of fact, the play is calling me right now. Hold up bro, it's Black, let me answer this right quick," Choyce said as he stood to his feet and walked off to the side.

I got up and headed to the Daytona Beach Pier. It was super fat on the other side of it and looked like five different block parties.

I stopped under the bridge because Channy crossed my mind. I had to call her.

"What's up, babe, how you feelin?" I questioned as I took a seat in the sand.

"I'm fine, just mad at you," she replied and sounded down.

"For what, what did I do, babe?" I questioned.

"Because, how the fuck you wait until I get

shot, to plan a trip for Miami? That shit ain't coo at all. I need you here with me, so get on the first plane back here now!" she demanded with an attitude.

"You better not be talking to them half-naked bitches down there either! I'll catch a flight my damn self, bullet wound and all, just to beat the shit out of all y'all," she went on to say.

I was lost for a second and didn't know what to say until I heard her laugh.

"Boy, I was just playing with you. I am mad, but not like that," she said.

"Wow, you had me about to start packing my shit up to catch a flight asap," I joked. I wiped the sweat from my forehead then sat back down.

"Nah, for real. Are you enjoying yourself?" she questioned in the sweet tone, I was used to hearing.

"Nah, I'm able to clear my mind, but I miss you like crazy. Don't worry, I'll plan something for us. I just need for you to heal up because we have plans," I assured her as I looked over and saw Choyce motion for me to come back.

"You'd better but go ahead and enjoy yourself. Relax, babe, everything is going to be okay. Thanks for checking on me. I love you."

"I love you too." After I hung up, I went over to see what Choyce wanted.

"What's the move, bro?" I questioned.

"It's lit, Black just told me he blessed us with a room at the Daytona Beach Regency. We got plenty of bottles and V.I.P. passes to a Moneybagg and Fivio Foreign concert," Choyce rejoiced as we shook up.

"Off top, I'm glad we already hit the mall up. Fuck it, we lit, let's fuck they heads up then," I geeked.

*****

We made it to the room. It had three bedrooms and a very spacious living room with plenty of furniture.

"Yo, this the type shit I'm looking forward to once I get to the league!" I said when we walked in and looked around.

"Nah, for real," Choyce agreed and sat down on the couch.

"Look, lil' bruh, I know you married and shit, but I'm not, and I gotta have some bitches up here tonight. I'm just letting you know right now," Choyce explained as he stood up and took his bags to his room.

After we got fresh, we applied our drip for the concert. I felt blessed on some king shit once I looked in the mirror. Choyce and I had a unique aura that kept all eyes on us. Whenever we stepped on the scene-- individually and collectively--we just stood out. Seeing us once again in that light, only made the moment more surreal.

"Come on, bro. Let's pregame right quick. It's too much drink in here to be on some lame shit," Choyce suggested as we popped a couple bottles of Glee Champagne and drunk a fifth of Remy Martin.

We left out of the hotel with two cases of Glee Champagne and a couple bottles of Remy. We were late but still found a nice spot in the V.I.P. section to set up for the concert.

"Watch this, lil' bruh," Choyce said as he found a group of bad ass bitches and handed them a couple bottles of Glee.

Whatever he was on, worked because we were surrounded by bad ass vibes all night. The concert was heat. Moneybagg and Fivio Foreign were on some lit shit.

*****

"Yo! Nigga! The fuck just happened?" I questioned once we made it back to the room.

"That's that rich nigga life, lil' bruh. We haven't seen it on this level, so it's new to us, but get used to it. Once you make it to the NFL, this is all we're going to know.

I agreed and was about to walk to my room to call Channy when I heard a knock on the door.

"Who is it?" I asked, not knowing we were expecting anyone.

"It's me, papi, open the door." As I opened the door it was the seven long haired, brown-skinned, sexy, half-naked Puerto-Rican women from the concert.

"Damn, y'all was serious," Choyce said as he pulled out some bands, and they walked in.

He grabbed the remote and had that Fivio

Foreign's *Big Drip* playing. Them bitches started acting bad to it. I walked in my room to call Channy.

"What's good, babe?" I questioned with a slur.

"Nothing, just woke up. Where you at?" she questioned.

"I'm at the room with bro," I said as I laid back on my bed.

"The room? I thought you said you was at a resort?" she questioned as if I'd lied to her.

"Nah, Choyce's guy got us a room for after the concert, so we wouldn't have to drive all the way back to our shit," I explained.

"So, why are you in the other room, while all them loud ass mothafuckahs is partying and shit! You must think I'm dumb or something!" she yelled then hung up the phone.

I didn't understand why she went off and that shit made me upset.

"The fuck would I have to lie for?" I questioned as I looked at my phone in anger. She then called me back on facetime.

169

"Hello?" I answered with aggression.

"Open the door and show me, who's all is in there with yo lying ass!" she demanded.

"Nah, babe, you don't want to see this shit," I answered in all honesty, but she insisted.

When I opened the door, one of the bitches was going from the splits, onto her back, and put her legs behind her head. A few of them were twerking on bro, some were freaking each other.

One was closer to my door, and she tried to garb me by the back collar of my shirt.

"Bitch, back up!" I demanded then walked back in my room and shut the door.

"Is that what you wanted you see?" I questioned. I was heated because she didn't give me the benefit of the doubt. But I understood were she was coming from because ain't no telling what I would've done if the shoe was on the other foot.

She just didn't know I'd rather talk to her on the phone than let them random ass bitches entertain me. She just didn't get it.

"Okay, that's how you wanna paly it, just think about how your car is going to look after I pick it up tomorrow. I can't believe you would do me like this." She busted out into tears and hung up the phone.

I called back, but she had me blocked.

"The fuck is wrong with her?" I questioned as I laid my phone on the bed.

I laid back as my liquor started to control my thoughts. I was about to just say fuck it but I closed my eyes instead. Channy was my queen. She had a lifetime of riches to offer me. I couldn't sacrifice that for one night of cheap thrills.

*****

It was five o'clock, and I was awakened out my sleep by one of my nightmares. I walked into the living room and it looked like a hurricane hit it. It was it was bitches, money, bottles, and empty condom wrappers everywhere.

"Bro, you wild as fuck," I said as shook my head and walked to his room. He sat at the edge of the bed in a bath towel while on the phone.

171

"What you on, bro?" I questioned, and he just held up one finger.

"Nah, we still here," he said.

"Alright, we on our way down. Come on, lil' bruh," he said as he got up and walked out the room.

"Aye! Wake up! It's time for y'all to get the fuck out!" he demanded then walked to the front door and unlocked it for them.

"Okay, papi," one of them said as she hurried to grab some money and her belongings. She then woke the rest up to do the same.

"So, what's the move?" I questioned once we were alone.

"I don't know, Black need for us to ride with him right quick," was all he said as he rushed to get dressed.

"Say less, lets ride." We walked outside and saw Black parked out front in a 2020 Rolls Royce Wraith.

We got in the back with him, and I could see why he called himself Black. If it were nighttime, all I would've seen was his jewelry. His drip game was sick with it though.

"What's going on with you?" Black asked with his heavy Jamaican accent as we got in.

"Not shit, chillin hard, what's up with you?" Choyce replied as we shook up with him.

"I'm good, who's them girls over there?" Black questioned and pointed. It was the ones we had up in the room. They waved and blew kisses at Choyce as the driver pulled off.

"Those are the vibes I met at the concert last night. By the way, thanks for the room. My brother and I had a good time in there," Choyce said in appreciation.

"No problem, it was the least I could do," he said as he finished rolling his blunt.

"Off top, so what's the play? You said that once I complete it, I'd be set for life, right?" I heard Choyce question. Bro was unpredictable, although he had good intentions for inviting me. There was no telling what he really went to Miami to do. But once I noticed the all gold AK 47s on the seat next to Black, I knew bro had a method to his madness.

"I'm a man of my word, you'll be set for life. Now, open your ears and hear me now. The amount of disrespect, in this city, is something that I just won't tolerate. That's the mission I have for you," he said in a demanding tone as he lit up his blunt.

"I understand, I deal with the same shit back home, so say less. Let's ride out."

Black's driver headed to the location while he talked to us the entire time.

"Listen man, these dudes are a bunch of envious men. They're our enemies, and I want you to kill them. Fuck all the talking. We have no time to waste, just kill them all at once. Element of surprise is a mufuckah. This is my new car, so they won't see you coming from a mile away," He explained as he looked at Choyce eye to eye.

We pulled up to the location as Black pointed them out.

"Let me tell you something, not everyone that smiles in your face likes you. Mi want him, him, and him ded rite bumbaclot now! Dem Bad mind mad kaaz mi big time now," Black demanded as his true Jamaican side came out.

"Try to take what's mine to make themselves big time. They will die today because of their envy. Their souls are vexed with jealousy, now go on," Black said as he clenched his blunt between his lips then handed Choyce the AK 47 with an extendo.

Choyce got out and handled that shit. He ran up close enough to shoot everybody Black pointed out, until the clip was empty. He got back in the car and the driver smashed off.

*****

We pulled back up to the hotel...

"Now, go. You two need to leave Florida and never come back. Mi gat it from here, de nex time wi will see each oda ah inna Jamdung," Black explained as said the next time we'd see again would be in Jamaica.

"And I will keep my promise. You and your brother are good for life."

"Nah, for real, and you got the address, so make it make sense," Choyce said. \

We made it back up to the hotel room.

"It's time to go get your shit together, so we can hit the highway." Choyce said.

We got packed up and went back to our resort home.

*****

"Chance, let me talk to you right quick," Choyce said as I was in the living room on the couch with my eyes closed in deep thought.

"I hear you when you tell me you feel as if you're haunted. I just want you to imagine how I feel," he said as he sat next to me.

"The only way, I can deal with my demons is to do more dirt. The more I do, the less I think about the bad things, I have done. It's like I'm trapped, bro. I get scared sometimes, but this is the life I chose," he explained.

"I don't want this for you, but bro, if you have to defend yourself, I'd want for you to be the one that came out on top. I never told you this, but thanks for having my back all them times," Choyce finished as we shook up, and he walked off.

Choyce never explained things fully, he

talked in parables. So, I just always took what applied to me and ran with it.

We rested up for a day then went back to Daytona Beach. I stood at the shoreline and over-looked the ocean. Choyce was in too deep as if he were in the middle of the Atlantic, and there was nothing I could do to save him.

Channy then crossed my mind. I couldn't believe her. Why would she not believe me? Even though I didn't do anything, I had to make it up to her. I turned to go sit down under our tent when I saw a group of girls walking my way. The sun shined bright behind them, so I couldn't see anything but their silhouettes.

The one that led the way was headed straight towards me, that's when I noticed the arm sling.

"Hell, nah," I said as I busted out laughing.

"Nah, nigga, don't laugh now!" Channy yelled out and got in my face.

"Get'em, girl!" one of her friends said.

The way the sun shined; it complimented her beautiful, caramel skin tone. She wore her hair long, and

177

the wind blew it across her pretty face. Her eyes changed from chestnut brown to hazel in the summer, but I'd been noticed that years ago. I always loved to look at her lips, they were so full beautiful and complimented her smile. Her legs were short thick and sexy and fit perfectly with her height and build.

She had on a sexy one-piece swimsuit and even had an arm sling to match. I could tell she made it; she was talented in fashion design.

"Chill out, babe, this is all a misunderstanding," I said as she backed me all the way up until my feet were in the water.

"Yeah, you thought I was playing when I said I'd be up here, didn't you? Sling and all, now where them, nasty ass triflin bitches you had up in that room the other night?" she fussed. I just couldn't keep a smile off my face.

She'd really flown all the way to Miami in her condition just to check me. I didn't even do shit though. The entire time she talked, I had my hand up to block the sun from my eyes.

"What's so funny? And take your hand down when you're talking to me!" she demanded.

"Look, babe. I'm telling you, I didn't do anything. I didn't entertain none of that shit the other night. That was Choyce's bright idea, you gotta believe me," I explained as I held my hands in the air as if I surrendered.

"Why Chance! Why should I believe you! Like, I told you niggas ain't shit!" She turned her back, and I couldn't do nothing but put my hands around her waist.

"Just chill, babe. I love you and wouldn't jeopardize what we have for no other woman on this earth. You are all I know," I assured her. she stepped away then turned around with a smile on her face. I then saw Choyce walk up out of nowhere. He was laughing so hard, he couldn't even stand up.

"What's going on?" I questioned. It seemed like everyone was in on the joke but me.

"Bro, here, take your phone. You left it at the resort, and it almost got me killed." Once he handed it to me, I could already tell what happened. She had followed my location.

"Bro, they had me cornered, asking me why I had all them freaky hoes around you and shit. Don't worry, she know you did the right thing," Choyce said as he continued to laugh.

"Yep, I pulled up your location and was on my way. You lucky I caught the earliest flight. If I would've been able to come up to that room, all y'all would've been dead," she threatened. I just shook my head.

"Babe, you're out here looking good as fuck right now. You got your hair done, nails and feet looking all pretty and shit. I would be stupid as hell to lose you," I said, then gave her a kiss.

"Why thank you, sir, and you're looking like my favorite kinda chocolate your damn self. Put a shirt on, nigga," she joked then we walked away along the beach.

"So, do yo really think I would do you like that?" I questioned as I had my arm around her waist.

"I mean, how would you act if I were out of town, and I told you one thing, but it was something different when you called?" she said as she looked down at the sand like she was ashamed, I had to see her crazy side, for free.

"I'm not going to lie, I would've caught a flight myself. You think you're crazy about me. But I'm crazy about you too, love," I said with a grin.

I was just glad to see that I had a rider on my team. She was just as down for me as I was for her. That's all I needed to help me cope with this crazy world. Channy and her friends were excited to spend the rest of the week with us at the resort and even more geeked when they heard we were taking a PJ back home.

*****

Leaving Orlando, heading home…

On are way home while the girls were sleep, I got a chance to talk with Choyce about the play I'd came up with for him.

"Bro, I need you to talk to you about something," I said as I sat next to him.

"What's good, bro?" he questioned as he took out his ear pods.

181

"How much money do you really have?" I asked.

Choyce was my twin brother, but we were the exact opposite. I had a strong business mind, and Choyce always had a knack to make money ever since we were kids. I knew it was only a matter of time before Choyce ran out of hiding spots for the money, he made. So, I introduced him to a better way.

"To tell you the truth, I stopped counting after one-hundred thou. I just know where it all is, and how it was stacked when I left it. Why'd you ask, bro?"

"I think it's time for you to invest, there's no sense in just having money in various spots if you don't have it invested in assets," I explained and had all his attention, so I continued.

"Bro, this world is all about assets and liabilities. Instead of us having to rent a private jet, why not figure out a way to buy our own? We got the drip, clothes, a couple car but those depreciate value, which makes them our liabilities," I said as I scrolled through my phone to pull something up.

"You have enough money to buy houses, buildings, things of that nature, and those would be our assets. It's also called equity, things that add value and worth. What you need is called a paper trail. If you have deeds and slips for legit properties and businesses, there's nothing the feds could come for, one day," I explained to Choyce as I found what I was looking for on my phone.

"Here it is, bro, there's ah public hearing coming up. I want us to go. We'll just see what we could make happen from there," I finished, and the look on his face was if he'd seen a ghost.

"It's crazy, you bought this up. Black was just asking me if I had access to a library. He said something about sending packages there."

"I was just trying to brainstorm a way to talk a librarian into helping make that happen."

"Plus, Muhammad told me the car garage, I had our cars remodeled in, is going out of business. I didn't even think of it until now, but I could buy both and flip the fuck out of the garage. Then, I'd open something like a private library. That's the move, lil' bruh. That's exactly the direction I need to head in life. Thank you."

That was music to my ears; I only had a couple months left until I went off to school. To see Choyce had more options for himself while I was gone, helped to ease my mind.

Chapter 8

The Public Hearing

"Choyce, as you already know, life isn't all about making money, but it's also about investing it. We are already kings, but in these days, we must be entrepreneurs for finical stability. What's the definition of an entrepreneur?" I questioned bro as we sat outside the public hearing.

"An entrepreneur is one that is willing to risk time and money in order to manage and maintain a business," Choyce recited. One thing about him was, he loved to read and study facts. He could read words and memorize their definition the first time.

"Off top, bro, but to add to it, an entrepreneur is also a person who organizes a business or businesses, taking on greater financial risks to do so," I shared.

"They both share similar meanings, but long story short, it all comes down to investing! Choyce, you are in a position that most grown men will never be in!" I further explained.

"You're smart, you have your high school diploma, and driver's licenses. You have a lot going on; all you're missing is businesses in your name, and they're right in this building for cheap. So, let's go."

"Off, top," bro agreed as we got out the car.

We had on casual clothes and looked presentable to do business. We walked inside the Public Hearing and immediately bought three houses in our neighborhood. Although we didn't see the car garage up for sale, we did find a library. The investment that I was most proud of was a night club called Big Fellas. It was the building right behind the car garage, we wanted down the street from our house.

Altogether, Choyce and I walked out that building with deeds, mortgage-backed certificates, land and bonds, for a little of nothing. We had a plan to hire contractors to upgrade our properties and business before the day ended.

"You see it now, bro? This is what the fuck I'm talking about, how does owning something make you feel?" I asked as soon as I got in the car.

"I can't lie, lil' bruh, this shit feels amazing," Choyce responded and looked over the paperwork.

"Man, thank you, but all of this is us, lil' bruh. You put in on this shit too. The money we hit off them couple licks, we pulled off, is part yours. You could've said no to anything I asked of you, but you chose to have my back. Now look at us, we businessowners on some boss shit."

I don't know why, but that was the first- time, I ever saw a tear almost fall from his eye. He was just a solid ass dude.

*****

I did my part in showing Choyce a different path. It didn't take long before he used his street smarts to extend his hustle.

"Hello? What's up, Black?" Choyce asked when he facetimed him. He looked skeptically at twelve wooden crates with fragile vintage books, stamped on all of them. They all sat in the front entrance of the library. That was the drop off location for his and Black's business.

The library looked like someone started to put some money into it but gave up on it. They left their tools behind and all. The front desk was new, and had plastic over it. The rest of it looked like it was just a bunch of wooden beams everywhere. All it needed was a little drywall, and it would've been good as new.

"Wah gwan brudah?" I heard Black respond.

"Not shit, I see you made good on your word," Choyce stated as he frantically looked out the window, to make sure the feds wasn't about to crash the spot.

"Yes, just like I told you, I would. I take it, you got my packages?" he said as if it were a normal-sized FedEx delivery. Choyce and I witnessed four people struggle, to get them in the front door.

"If the packages you're talking about, are these twelve crates, that are sitting in the middle of the floor," Choyce said as he switched his camera around on them then back on me, "then yeah, I got it. I damn near didn't accept it. Are these what the fuck I think they are?" he questioned, then looked over at me like what the fuck.

"That's what I promised you. What were you

expecting, something small and pretty with a ribbon on it?" he joked.

"Nah, nothing like that. I'm just making sure the way you sent this is safe?" Choyce's curiosity had gotten the best of him. It had me hoping the feds didn't rush in as soon as he opened them up.

"Du nah fret about it, mi would not have sent it. If I thought it would bring you more harm than good," Black explained.

"Say less then. I'm going to crack this bitch open and make sure I get it gone. We should be straight though, I mean, this first one is on you for the play I pulled in Miami, right?" Choyce had to check before he even touched it. I knew my bro; he wasn't playin no games. If it were something else going on other than what was discussed, then he wasn't going to take no part in it.

"Yes, wi ah gud all of them are paid for. You did a huge favor for me, more than what you know. And it's even something extra for you and your brother," Black said to make sure that Choyce knew it was a legit transaction.

189

"Off top, thanks for the lookout. Once again, it's good to know that you're a man of your word. That's very good for business," Choyce replied in acceptance.

"Not a problem, mi told yuh, dat I mean wat mi say. Just mek sure dat you and yuh brother. Mek it to Jamaica dis summer wid de extra money yuh mek. Big up, brother, I'm about to go. Talk to yuh later."

"Say less, in ah minute then," Choyce said and ended the call.

He knew this day was coming, so me made major power moves with aggression ever since we'd come back from Florida. His bossed-up status had been felt all over the city, just so no one tried him when he got in power.

"Chance, hand me that crowbar and a few of them thrash bags right quick," he asked while he observed where to open it from.

"Ight bet," I said and handed him the crowbar.

He pried it open and got all the bubble wrap and Styrofoam off the top. Then, he stopped to look inside like an illuminating light shined out of it.

"Oh, I see what he did, these mufuckahs is

laminated then vacuum-sealed to make them smell proof. But god damn, bro. Look at all these bricks!" Choyce rejoiced as he held up a couple.

All the bricks had thin book covers on them. The edges of the bricks even had wedges to give the illusion of vintage book pages. Black was a smart dude.

"So, now what, lil' bruh? This is a lot of money to be made, where do we go from here?" Choyce questioned.

"This is the easy part, bro. Now, that we got properties. You should use three of the houses and have mufuckahs in'em sellin bricks for you. Whoever occupies the houses, we'll put it in their names like renters. That would make it easier for you to get this shit off," I suggested as we finished breaking down the first crate.

"Off top, and since the money is all profit, we'll invest it back into the houses, this library, and the night club," Choyce added.

"That's the move, bro, but to start a legit paper trail. Once we sell a house or rent it out, we'll go back to the public hearing and buy more. We can monopolize this area and buy up every foreclosed home. That away, when you tell these fuck niggas this is your hood; you'll actually mean it," I further explained.

"Nah, for real, but I'm about to get to moving these bricks. We're going to take a trip to Jamaica, soon. Get ready to spend few weeks there, so you can enjoy the rest of your summer vacation," Choyce said as we shook up.

I took it upon myself and made calls to contractors. I made bids in the renovation of the library, night club, and rental properties. I struck a deal with a contractor within the first call.

*****

It took about two weeks, and Choyce and I were sitting in the lobby of our own night club as we brainstormed ideas of how to make a profit from it.

"I'm telling you, bro. We should turn this bitch into a strip club and call it Club Rated R," Choyce gave his opinion.

"Rated R would be a good name for a strip club, but we still have to think about our liquor license. And shit, nigga, we aren't even old enough to get in the club or buy liquor." I laughed.

"Could you imagine opening a strip club and promoting it all the way until the grand opening. And we couldn't even get into our own shit?" I said and laughed some more.

"Nah, for real," Choyce said and shared a laugh himself.

"On some real shit, let's make it an under twenty-one club," he suggested, and it made sense.

"Now you're talking, bro. We can call it club RED after our favorite color," I said.

"Yeah that, or club Bumbaclot," Choyce joked as he mocked his slime, Black. We fell out laughing.

"You sound goofy as fuck right now." I laughed so hard, I fell on the floor. He sounded just like that dude.

"Seriously though, he could promote concerts and shit. I know for sure, nights like that would have this bitch lit as fuck!" Choyce went on to say.

"Say less, it's lit then."

*****

A couple days later, Choyce and I met up with a contractor for the finishing touches on our club. He met us around noon to introduce ourselves. Right after we shook hands Choyce, went in.

"Yo, check this out, we named the club RED. So off top, we want a sign with a cold ass logo that spells RED on the front of the building. I want it to be so big, mufuckahs should be able to see it from the highway," Choyce demanded.

"We want smaller club logos on the back walls of the front and backstage, with red lighting all through that bitch. We also want the same smaller logos on the walls in the up and downstairs VIP booths, beverage stations, and DJ booths," he continued. The contractor couldn't write it all down fast enough. I couldn't help but to laugh.

"Fuck it, put logos above all the fire exits and in our office space. We want a fireproof, drop box safe, that's big enough to hold hundreds of thousands of dollars. I want a remote to make that bitch come up out the floor and go back in it. Make sure it's a combination safe too and put it in the far-right corner of our office," Choyce said.

"Are you finished?" I questioned as I wiped the tears off my cheeks from laughter. I just never saw him in that business-minded light before.

"Nah, lastly, we want an elevator that goes from the first to second floor. And oh, yeah, we need this done in a week," Choyce finished with his high list of demands.

"Well, if the money is right, he'll have it done for you, that's not a problem," the contractor agreed.

*****

Grand Opening

Choyce and I woke up early to go look at the club.

"Tonight's our grand opening, lil' bruh. I see dreams come true every day," Choyce said as we stood in front of the building.

The contractor had us a cold ass Club RED logo design in cursive. It was big but not an eye sore.

"I'm just glad that we hired the right people. They really payed attention to the detail," I commented as we walked in with confidence.

"So, what's the play?" Choyce questioned as we want over a few things before we opened the doors up and made sure everything met our expectations.

"We'll have security at the front entrance, spread out on the dance floor, and in all our blind spots, fire exits and all to make sure no bullshit pops off tonight," I explained.

"The mainstage is forty feet from the front door. The DJ booth is to the left of it and on the right, a total of four VIP spaces. Backstage is like a mini club with plenty of space for whoever that pays for it and their entourage."

"We have plenty of wall-mounted sofas and sofa chairs throughout the entire club, up and downstairs to accommodate everyone," I said as we walked onto the elevator.

"The upstairs has our own personal VIP right next to our office. Our office does a half-circle overviewing the club with dark bulletproof tinted windows, giving us a panoramic view of our business. We can see down on anybody, but they can't see up to us," I concluded as we entered our office.

"Fuck it then, we lit, bro. I done got used to this already," Choyce said as he sat in one of our executive chairs and kicked his feet up on our office desk. It's was costumed designed and faced the front door and safe.

"Yeah, we did our thing with this, it's amazing what we can pull off when we cohesively collaborate on one accord," I said as I sat in the executive chair next to his.

"We do it every time, let's go get fresh, lil' bruh. A first impression is a lasting one. We about to bring the city out," Choyce suggested.

"Off top, we're going to have them talking about this shit forever," I said in agreement.

*****

Doors open.

We had the doors opened since eight

197

o'clock, and as I looked down from the office, the DJ had everyone turned the fuck up. Security were doing their job while Choyce collected money.

"So far, so good," I said to myself as I sat back down. I was waiting on Channy to pull up. I had a gift for her and couldn't wait to see her reaction.

"Lil' bruh, I know you're not going to stay in this office all night, are you? I'm down there collecting money, politickin and makin, it happen," Choyce said as he made the first drop in the safe.

"Nah, I was just enjoying the fact that we have our own establishment. It's a wonderful feeling to see everybody lit like this. What's the body count so far?" I asked as Choyce walked over to the window.

"We're filled up and can't let anybody else in if we wanted to. But guess who showed up?" Choyce said as he pointed in our lower VIP section.

"That's exactly who I was looking for. Damn, she's lookin good as fuck too," I said, geeked up when I saw Channy and a few of her friends.

"I knew you were, that's way I gave her a VIP

booth. Let's go live in the moment, lil' bruh." We walked out the office like dons.

We locked up the office and got on the elevator. Once we got off, all eyes were on us--the men of the hour. We were fitted up, drip game was stupid, and we had an aura that couldn't be fucked wit. Choyce got called over to his slime, and I headed over to VIP.

"What's good, babe!" I yelled out over the music and couldn't help my proud grin as I stood in front of her.

"Oh, my God, babe. This place is live as fuck! I'm so proud of you!" she rejoiced then gave me a hug. She smelled good, and her body was so soft I didn't want to let go.

"Thank you, babe, but I'm glad you're here to share this moment with me," I said as I looked her over.

She had on a see-through bodycon dress with the long vee cut down to her stomach. I could see her nipple covers and thong perfectly. She had on a diamond choker with another thinner diamond necklace that dripped between her boobs down her stomach and some Gucci boots with the hand purse to match.

"As you can see, I'm with my hittas. And they came to get lit, but I came for that dick, zaddy," she said as she grabbed it. I had to laugh because she was just crazy for free. I loved that about her.

"Shiid, we can go in my office right now, bullshit ain't nothing," I joked back but was serious if she were wit it.

"Y'all should come to the upstairs VIP with me," I suggested and pointed over to the elevator.

"Sure, do you have any smoke up there?" Channy asked, and it made me do a doubletake.

"Yeah, plenty, but I didn't know that you smoked though." I had one eyebrow raised as she erased all my curiosities with her devilish grin.

"Zaddy, it's a lot you don't know about me yet. Come on, girls, we're going to the upstairs VIP," she said and led the way like she was a runway diva.

"But we're already in VIP, and who is he?" one of her friends, I hadn't met yet, said with an attitude.

"Bitch, the nigga wit the smoke, so let's go," someone else replied and looked at her like, *just keep your mouth shut, I'm trying to get high.*

"What kind of smoke? Because I'm not going up there to be smoking on some bunk shit," she said as if she was highly annoyed, but I could tell it was all for some attention.

"Well, stay the fuck down here! You doin too much. Come on y'all, let's see what the upstairs talking about," Channy demanded.

"Period, bitch," someone else said.

"Follow me." I laughed.

"Girl, you didn't tell me him and his twin own this place. You better keep him," I heard her friend whisper as they entered the elevator.

I just smiled and put my arm around Channy as I pressed the up button. Everyone got out accept Channy and me.

"So, where's this office of yours?" she said as the doors closed, and she pushed me back against the elevator wall.

She kept steady eye contact with me as she unfastened my belt. She reached her hand in my pants and felt I was already hard. I wanted to fuck the shit out of her right then and there.

I had to be easy with her because of her shoulder, when I turned her around and pinned her against the wall.

"Oh yes, babe. You're getting me so wet right now," she moaned as I kissed the side of her neck because I knew it was her spot. The smell of her perfume had me in paradise. I grabbed one of her legs and held it on my side.

"You really wanna take this to my office?" I questioned before I was about to put it in.

"Yes, babe, this has me so turned on right now," she replied with passion. I let go of her leg and adjusted my belt back.

"It's right over, here," I said in a seductive manner, but as soon as I stepped out, I saw Choyce surround by some niggas as they talked loudly.

"Hell, nah. Girl, we about to go back downstairs," one of her friends said as they were about to rush back into the elevator.

"Hold up y'all, just go in the VIP right quick," I said, but they didn't budge out of fear.

I knew they didn't have any weapons because security checked at the door, but I still didn't like what I saw.

"What them niggas over there talking about, Chance?" one of my security guards said after he ran up the back stairs, with a money bag in his hand to make another drop.

"I don't know but take them to the VIP right quick. Put that jar on the table and some Swishers, so they can roll up. I'm ah go see what this is about," I said as I took the money bag.

"Be careful, babe," Channy said with concern as I headed towards Choyce. I noticed how he kept his composure. So, I knew he wasn't in danger, but I still had to check on him.

"You know, how me and my slimes get down out here! We don't fuck around when it comes to gettin to the money! We can handle whatever you put in our hands!" Dude said with strong hand gestures as I shoved through and stood next to Choyce.

"I'm the nigga that put all of you on, remember. I know how y'all move," Choyce said as he postured up with his hand in a fist.

Bro wasn't shaken at all as he reminded them of who he was and looked at dude, doin all the talking, eye to eye aggressively.

I noticed how they were sizing us up. They were checking out our drip too hard, and it didn't seem like they wanted to do business. So, I had to intervene.

"What's up wit these niggas, bro? Why they talkin all aggressive and shit?" I questioned as I stared hard at the nigga that mean mugged me.

"These them lil niggas, I used to have lined up at my locker everyday," Choyce explained as he looked over at me.

"Yeah, I remember them now, but what they on though?" I questioned because I didn't like their demeanor.

"I just wanna see how fast they can flip a couple kilos. These niggas sold a lot of zips for me in high school. So, I gotta know if they're ready to graduate, you feel me?" he said then looked back at them.

"Nah, for real. Put these lil' foot soldiers to work then," I said but still wasn't feeling their vibe.

"Yeah, we got a house for you and all. All y'all gotta do is post up and get to the money. That shouldn't be that hard at all." What Choyce explained made everyone stop all that tough shit and pay attention.

"And from what I remember, everything that y'all touch turns to gold. I'm just giving you all a chance to see if you still got it," Choyce continued to work his finesse game. I eased up because I didn't wanna fuck up his money.

"We appreciate this, but we already got our hood on lock. So, we'll just move it from there, and if it's like the shit that we had back then or better, then we shouldn't have no issues, you feel me?" dude questioned in a slick manner.

"Nah, I don't feel you. I don't give a fuck about what you got on lock or none of that. This shit I got is different. If you get this from me, you sell it where the fuck I say, and if you don't have my money when I come for it, it's going to be some problem's. Now, do you feel me?" Choyce stated as he pointed all four of his fingers in dude's face.

Once I saw he had the situation under control, I went to put the drop in the safe then headed to the VIP room.

"Hold up, lil' bruh," Choyce said as he caught up with me.

"I saw you walking out of the elevator with your queen. What's up with the thick one that was at the beach though?" Choyce questioned.

"She's in here, bro, come in and shoot your shot." As we entered the VIP, I told my security guard that he could go back and watch the floor.

"Where have you been, babe, I missed you?" Channy questioned as she walked up to give me a kiss.

"Nah, for real. I couldn't wait to get back in here with you. I gotta gift for you outside," I said as I took her by the hand.

I looked over and saw Choyce shooting his

shot at her friend. So, I knew it was the perfect time to give it to her.

"Oh, I like gifts," she said as I led the way.

We walked out the VIP and headed to the back staircase. Once we made it down to the exit door, I turned to brief her.

"Channy, I love you more than you could ever imagine. I'm in a different position in life now. So, I wanted to share my blessings with you," I said as I opened the door.

"Oh, my God!" she screamed and ran out towards it.

"Oh, my God! I can't believe you did this for me. Thank you, babe! Oh, my God this is real!" she rejoiced.

"Ever since we rode in it on our prom night. You talked so highly about it, that I just had to get you one. I thought, I would've had to wait until I got drafted to the league, but the opportunity presented itself a little sooner," I said as I tossed her the key.

"Oh, my God, I got a G-Wagon! What the

fuck!" she said, then jumped in my arms.

"Thank you, babe, I love you so much," she said. She looked me in my eyes and kissed all on my face.

I got her a pink 2020 G-Wagon decked out with the dark tents and pink Forgi rims. Muhammed had the deals on the cars, that's how Choyce got ours. Once I found out, I had bro give me some money from the couple licks I'd pulled off with him. That's how I got that for her.

"I love you too." Her excitement was a thrill to my heart. She just didn't know what she meant to me. I was thankful she came into my life.

"I wanted to do something else for you, but it was already sold by the time I saw it," I mentioned as I stood by her while she was in the driver's seat.

"Something like what?" she questioned while a stream of tears fell from her eyes.

"I wanted to buy you your own boutique. I saw the perfect location and everything right around the corner from your house," I said.

"Wow, you wouldn't believe this but, I'm the

one that bought it. It was either that or an older model G-Wagon. I walked out on faith and chose the boutique, and now, look at God," she explained.

I knew her story and to had personally seen her make outfit after outfit, for all the years I had known her. The fact that she was so cold with it and made onlookers think she had her own personal designer. When I heard her say, she had taken her talent to the next level on her own, it gave me tears of joy.

"Congratulations, babe, you deserve it," I said as I leaned in and kissed her on the forehead.

"Well thank you, sir. I named it Channy Nicole, that's my brand name. But since you were going to purchase a building for me, why don't you just supply it for me? I mean, I already bought everything I need in my head, I just need the money to bring it into fruition," she said with a serious face, but I knew her sense of humor.

"Yo, you be having me weak as fuck, Channy." I laughed

"What?" she questioned.

"That *you already bought everything you need in your head* part was the one. You got it babe, tell me how much you need, and I'll make it happen. Just be sure I'm VIP at your grand opening too," I said as she got out, and we hugged.

"Hold on, babe, this is Unique facetimein me," she said then answered.

"Um, I'm riding home with him. So, you can take my car, I'll just come pick it up in the morning, okurr?" her friend said. I just smiled because I knew Choyce worked his move.

"Where are you two going, hoe? And, nah, because I'm driving my own shit, bitch. Okay? Period," Channy said in a joking manner.

"Your own shit? Bitch, let me see." Channy took a step back and went into a slow spin as she let out a long biiiiitch all the way until the G-Wagon was in camera view.

All I heard was Unique screaming at the top of her lungs.

"Girl! Come look at Channy's new ride!" I

heard her yell followed by even more screaming.

"Yes, scream at the rich bitch. I'm the shit, I know," Channy joked and hung up. She then took pics to post on all her social media. She connected to Bluetooth and played her favorite rapper, Megan Thee Stallion's song *Freak Nasty*.

Channy twerk game was stupid. I always loved to watch her dance especially when she was lit. She paused the song and stopped.

"Nah, but seriously though, do you feel like following me home? I just got this bad feeling out of nowhere," Channy questioned as she looked up at me.

"I got you, babe, pull me around to my car," I said as I hopped in on the passenger side.

It was so much traffic after the club had let out. It took us forever to get to my car. By the time we did, Choyce was already standing by his.

"Aye, bro. I'm about to follow her home," I said as I got out, and we shook up.

"Where she stay, bro?" he questioned as if he were worried.

"On 46th Street not too far from here," I answered, not knowing why everyone seemed so uneasy.

"Bet, I'm headed that way, so Unique can park her shit. Meet me at that Shell's gas station before you head back home," Choyce said as I got in my car and followed Channy.

"Be careful, lil' bruh," Choyce said before I completely pulled off.

I didn't know what the look in his eyes meant. I couldn't tell if he was proud of me or worried about me, but I never saw it before.

I felt like everyone was buggin out. When I looked up through my sunroof at a stoplight, something seemed different about the moon. I brushed it off because was too caught up in the moment to sky watch, like I usually did. Right then, Channy called my phone. I could her playing Yo Gotti's *Like That* low in the background.

"How you like the ride, babe?" I questioned.

"I love it, but I called to tell you thank you for, not letting me go to overboard when I approach you sexually. You just don't know how much that turns me on and makes me want you even more," she said as she slowed her speed so we could cruise.

"You're welcome, babe. I just know it's something that we've never done before. I want our first time to be special. I feel like if we would've had sex already, that misunderstanding back in Miami would've ruined us," I said as we turned onto her block.

"Yeah nigga, cause if you think that I'm crazy now, just wait until you put that big ass monster in me. You ain't seen nothing yet." She laughed as she pulled into her driveway. I pulled in behind her and got out, so I could walk her to the door.

"I love you, babe, but I gotta meet Choyce at the gas station around the corner. He should be about to pull up," I said as and made sure she was safely at her door. I then gave her a kiss.

"Okay, babe, be safe. I love you too and call me when you make it home."

On my way back to my car, I wished that was our home, that we'd pulled into the driveway of. That away, I wouldn't have had to leave her, I could've just stayed.

Choyce called me as soon as I got into my car.

"Where you at, lil' bruh?" he questioned.

"About to go up to the Shells on 46th I have to get some gas anyway," I answered. As smooth as my night went, I just couldn't see why Choyce and Channy had them bad vibes.

"Nah, for real. I need to get some my damn self. Wait for me, I'm about to pull up," Choyce said.

I pulled into the gas station and parked at the pump. Choyce walked up to my driver's side window, so I let it down.

"Bro, Unique freak nasty! Nigga, she just wrapped a fruit roll up around my dick then sucked the candy off and my nut out in ten seconds," he said and laughed so hard, he had to use my car door to stand up.

"No shit? Bro, that's freaky as fuck!" I said and shared a laugh with him.

"I haven't pumped my gas yet, so give me your money. I'm going in," Choyce went on to say.

I gave bro my money, and as I watched him walk into the gas station, out of nowhere my car door opened.

214

My eyes closed when I heard the first gunshot, followed by two more. My body went limp, and I couldn't open my eyes all the way. I'd been shot three times; I just didn't know where.

I got pulled out my car and everything was so blurry as I hit the ground. I just heard the horsepower of my Demon muscle on its way out of the gas station lot. My ears rung, and I heard someone tell me to keep still and don't move.

To be continued…

To submit a manuscript to be

considered, email us at

submissions@majorkeypublishing.com

Be sure to <u>LIKE</u> our Major Key

Publishing page on Facebook!

be obtained

∠0
2B/1524